MERRY LITTLE SUGAR RUSH

Snowflake Falls, book 2

USA Today Bestselling Author

Lacey Black

Merry Little Sugar Rush

Snowflake Falls Series, book 2

Copyright © 2025 Lacey Black
Cover Design by Y'all. That Graphic.
Editing by Kara Hildebrand

Proofreading by Sandra Shipman, Joanne Thompson, and Karen Hrdlicka

Format by Brenda Wright, Formatting Done Wright

ISBN-13: 978-1-951829-69-8

Chapter One

Joy

I'm up before my alarm, excitement racing through my veins.

Today is the start of the Christmas season, and I am here for it.

I am pumped.

I am ready.

I spent all afternoon and evening yesterday transforming my little bakery and coffee shop into a winter wonderland for today. It's December first, the day we officially kick off the holiday season in our small town.

Snowflake Falls, a beautiful little town nestled in the Rocky Mountains in Colorado, is home to twenty-eight hundred people. Most of us were born and raised here, and all of us lovers of all things Christmas.

I grew up celebrating the holidays spectacularly. For the entire month of December, our town is brimming with Christmas spirit. We've been dubbed one of the premiere holiday family destinations for the last eighteen years running, only losing out to some other random town in Indiana named after the big man in the red suit.

Not very original, if you ask me...

But our love for the holidays is woven into the very fabric of our quaint little town. The entire month of December is a celebration, from the Miss Snowflake Falls pageant to the weekly carnivals and family-focused events. Every business decorates, every house, every streetlight. The entire community digs deep into their Christmas spirit, and there's nowhere else I'd rather be. My entire family lives and breathes this glorious holiday-infused mountain air.

I move through my morning routine easily, getting ready for work and drinking a strawberry and banana protein smoothie. I could easily wait until I get to work and enjoy some of the sweet treats and gourmet coffee drinks I craft, but then I'd likely weigh twice as much as I do now and be on the verge of diabetes.

Don't get me wrong. I taste.

A lot.

I am only human, after all, but I try to keep it in check.

My pride and joy is The Sweet Escape, a quaint little bakery and coffee shop in the middle of our downtown square. Ever since I received my first Easy-Bake Oven at the age of seven, I knew what I wanted to do with my life.

It wasn't easy though. I worked at our small grocery store through high school and during my two years at junior college. I started off as a cashier before the bakery attendant retired, leaving me to make cookies and donuts daily. I loved it, even if I always felt like it could be more. The owners of the grocery store didn't feel the need to expand, however, so I was always limited on what I could offer the public, despite the fact their cake and pastry sales were up considerably.

In addition to working at the grocery store, I continued to bake pies and cakes for community bake sales and church gatherings. People were purchasing my lemon loaves under the table, handing me cash like I was dealing something inappropriate. I was their sugar dealer, and I haven't looked back since.

When I hit twenty-five, it was time. Mom and Dad own a larger building in downtown, where her hair salon is housed. When they purchased it years ago, they divided the space in half, converting it into two smaller businesses instead of one larger one. She had rented the other area to an insurance company, and when the agents reached retirement age, they stepped away from their business and closed.

That meant the second space was empty, and my dream of owning my own bakery was within my grasp.

It took a lot of hard work and even more start-up capital. I had been saving every penny I made, in hopes of one day achieving the dream I strived toward. I even lived at home longer than I should have, again, so I could scrimp and save. When I reached twenty-three, I think my parents were searching for a way to finally enjoy their golden years without one of their daughters still underfoot, so they transformed the upstairs space above the businesses into an apartment for me.

It's actually a decent little living space, since the upstairs wasn't divided the way the downstairs was. There's a large bedroom, bathroom, and open concept kitchen and living room. There's also plenty of storage, both in the apartment and outside of it, since Mom has always used it for that purpose.

But the best part about my cute little apartment is the fact I work right down the stairs. It takes me seconds to get there, and I don't even have to go outside, since the steps are located inside the building. Of course, I still go out when I place my first batch of goodies in the oven. We get a lot of snow here, so between shoveling and salting the walkway, I make sure the approach to my business is cleaned off the best I can.

A quick glance out the window confirms we got more snow last night. I love the snow. There's nothing more beautiful than your entire town being blanketed in fluffy, glistening white snow, especially during the holidays. Twinkle lights seem to twinkle even brighter when they're covered with snow, and coffee seems to taste even better when you're watching it fall from the comfort of warmth and coziness.

That's what I try to offer at The Sweet Escape.

I hum "Jingle Bells" as I give myself a final once-over in the bathroom mirror and make my way downstairs. I inhale the sweet scent of sugar and cinnamon, reveling in the smells of the holidays before I even have the rear entrance to the bakery open. The moment I turn the key in the old knob, I inhale and smile.

My favorite season.

My favorite time of day.

The world around me is still sleeping, and I'm about to start creating something magical.

I turn on the speaker system that runs through the shop and let the sounds of the season fill the quiet. Nothing puts me in the holiday spirit like Christmas music, and as today officially kicks off the season for Snowflake Falls, I feel like nothing can dampen my mood. Not even the prospect of shoveling snow.

I spend the next hour prepping dough for pastries and donuts, and just as I slip the tray into the oven and set the timer, I hear a knock on my front door. Turning my attention that way, I walk to the door and smile when I see who's standing there.

Dad waves and holds up his shovel. Releasing the lock on the door, I say, "Good morning, Dad."

"Morning, baby girl," he replies, stepping inside the shop and giving me a gentle kiss on the cheek.

"What are you doing? I'm about to go out and take care of that," I insist.

Of course it falls on deaf ears though. Dad waves off my comment with his gloved hand. "I don't mind, sweetie. I came to get it all cleaned up for your mom and sister."

My mom's salon is next door, and my older sister, Eve, followed in her footsteps and became a beautician. Roxie works at the third station in the salon, and Mom mentioned a couple of weeks back she had an inquiry from another young woman who will be graduating from cosmetology school in a couple of months and would love to make The Beauty Studio her home.

"Thank you, Dad."

"You're welcome, sweetie."

"I'll get you a cup of coffee started," I offer.

"Appreciate it." He glances over my shoulder. "Whatcha put in the oven?" His eyes light up at the prospect of stealing a sweet treat for breakfast before I even open.

"Wednesday brings us caramel apple and cranberry cream cheese Danishes."

His green eyes practically sparkle with excitement. "I wouldn't mind one of those cranberry ones," he says with a big grin.

"I've got you," I reply with a wink.

"All right, I'll go get the walk cleared off and salted."

"Then come in and get warm."

He exits my shop, moving toward Mom's business first. My parents have the type of marriage everyone strives for. They both support each other regardless, and they're not afraid of PDA. Growing up, it was nauseating, but now that I'm older, I can appreciate the way they love and show love.

Maybe someday I'll be lucky enough to have that...

I watch him for a few moments before I'm interrupted by the chime of my kitchen timer. Leaving Dad to it, I return to the kitchen and remove my first batch of the morning pastries from the oven. When I have the next tray inside and the fresh batch cooling, I head back to the front area to make Dad's coffee. He prefers a regular brewed coffee with two sugars and creamer, so his order is fairly easy. Occasionally he'll indulge in something sweeter for the season, like a white chocolate cherry mocha or a crème brûlée latte, but usually that's when he's humoring either Mom, Eve, or me.

Just as I'm pouring his coffee into one of my The Sweet Escape biodegradable cups, the door behind me opens. "Got ya all cleaned up, sweetie," Dad says, letting the door close behind him.

Spinning around, I hand over his coffee. "Thank you."

He nods, taking his first sip of fresh brew. He makes a sound of pure satisfaction and smiles. "The best."

"Come on back. My next batch of pastries is about done, and the first ones should be cool enough to eat by now," I say, returning to my kitchen.

Dad follows willingly, his stomach leading the way. He moves over to the counter, away from my prep and workstation, and takes a seat on the stool. I feel his eyes on me as I retrieve a paper plate and slip a pastry on top. When I place it in front of him on the counter, he offers a warm smile. "You're my favorite baker daughter."

I can't help but snort. "And Eve is your favorite hairdresser daughter," I state, repeating what he's told me numerous times over the last few years and earning a laugh in return.

"That she is." Bringing the pastry to his mouth, he takes a hearty bite and grins as he chews. "Amazing, as always."

The timer announces the completion of my second set of pastries, so I return my attention to doing what needs done prior to opening the bakery. Dad remains seated in the corner, happily watching me work. He's done that many times, and honestly, I enjoy having him here.

I've always been a daddy's girl. My sister and Mom have always been close, even when we were young girls. Eve found so much pleasure in watching Mom work, always wanting to go with her to the salon. Me, on the other hand, went wherever Dad went, which was usually outside. I used to help him around the yard any chance I got, and we'd always end our time together with a visit to the snack shack at the tree farm for some hot cocoa and apple donuts.

"Did you hear about Dale Whitman yet?" Dad asks, pulling my attention away from the task at hand.

I turn his way, a wave of worry washing over me. "No, what happened?"

"He had a stroke," he informs me, a look of pure worry and anguish on his face.

My hands cover my mouth as I gasp. "What? No!"

He glances down, clearly upset about his good friend's health. "A couple of nights ago. Carol called me pretty late."

I move to where he sits and reach for his hand. "That's why you're up so early."

He shrugs, not arguing. "I was up, so I thought I'd get a jump on clearing sidewalks."

"I'm sorry, Dad. How is he?" I ask, thinking about the old man who's not only been my father's employer for more than a decade, but also a friend.

"They're waiting on the results of some testing, which they'll do today." He sighs loudly and shakes his head. "He's always been this larger-than-life presence, you know? It's hard to picture Whitmans' Tree Farm without him buzzing around on a tractor or harvesting pumpkins each fall."

My throat is thick and dry, and I find it hard to swallow. "I'm sure he'll be okay, Dad, and he'll be back on that tractor and picking pumpkins before you know it."

Whitmans' Tree Farm is an institution in Snowflake Falls. Not only is it a live tree farm, where you can cut down your own Christmas tree, but it's a family-friendly outing destination. They offer horse-drawn carriage rides, ornament making, carolers on Sundays, and so much more. Plus, they're open year-round with greenhouses, gardening supplies, and a pumpkin patch. I have as many memories at the tree farm as I do attending the festival. It's woven into my blood, into the genes of this very town.

"Well, at least Karl is still there. Plus, Sheila, Klint and Tasha," I say, referring to Dale's youngest son, daughter-in-law, and two of his grandkids. Not to mention Klint's wife, Gretchen, helps out often while their son, Noah, is in school. It truly is a family-run business.

He nods. "Yeah, but I don't think Gretchen will be much help for a bit. She fell on the ice a few days ago and messed up her knee. Plus, I'm sure Carol's going to be at the hospital while Dale is there, and Tasha has classes until closer to the holidays."

My heart drops in my chest. "I bet as soon as word spreads about Dale, you'll have more help than you know what to do with," I tell him reassuringly. That's one of the beautiful things about a small town. If someone needs help, there's usually a line of friends and townspeople ready to jump in.

"Yeah, I'm sure you're right," he replies, but his smile doesn't quite reach his eyes. I can tell he's upset, but also a little worried about work. This is their busiest time of year, and being down one or two employees can be pretty rough on a small business. "Well, I've yapped at you too long. You have a shop to open soon," he adds proudly, standing up and reaching for his coffee cup.

"Can I top that off for you before you go?" I ask, extending my hand.

He grins. "I wouldn't say no to that."

We step out into the main part of the bakery, and I refill his coffee, adding the right amount of sugar and cream before grabbing a lid and securing it to the top. "Here ya go." I don't miss the fact there's already a twenty in the tip jar for the day. That's one of the many arguments we've had over the years. I refuse to charge him or Mom, so they always make sure to overtip way more than the worth of what they ate or drank.

"Thanks, sweetie." He leans in and presses a kiss to my cheek. "Have a great day."

"You too," I tell him, walking him to the door.

He glances around and smiles. "This place looks beautiful. That tree is the perfect fit."

We picked out one of my trees together over the weekend, and he delivered it yesterday. I spent all evening decorating the bakery and still have to tackle my apartment upstairs. "It is," I confirm, loving how the tall, skinny tree fills the corner of the room without being in the way of any of the tables. "Keep me posted on Dale," I add as he slips his gloves back on and steps outside.

"I will, honey. Oh, and make sure you take your mom one of those Danishes. You know how she loves cranberries."

"I'll save her and Eve each one," I reply, even though I know my sister isn't a fan of cranberries. Yet, she always eats and enjoys whatever I make with them in it, which makes me secretly preen like a peacock.

"Love you," he hollers, grabbing his shovel and heading to where his truck is parked along the road.

"Love you more!" I reply with a wave.

The first peeks of sunlight are rising above the old buildings in our beautiful downtown square, shimmering off the glistening snow, but my heart is heavy. The Whitman family means so much to so many, myself included. My love for their tree farm isn't just because my dad has worked there for the last ten-plus years. I used to run those rows of trees and helped pick pumpkins growing up.

With Burk.

My oldest friend.

The one I haven't seen since he left town the summer after our eighth-grade year.

But now isn't the time to wonder what happened to an old friend. I have to finish preparing today's pastries, as well as get some loaves of bread ready. Not to mention I need to start baking gingerbread cookies and cake pops for this weekend. The bakery will be open prior to the start of the Miss Snowflake Falls Princess competition.

Lots to do and little time to do it in.

That still doesn't stop my brain from conjuring up an image of a lanky boy with braces and shaggy brown hair.

I wonder where Burk Whitman is in the world today...

Chapter Two

Burk

I stop my rental car at the entrance of the tree farm and take a deep breath. The gate is still closed for the morning, but it's the large sign hanging from the wooden archway that has my complete attention.

Whitmans' Tree Farm.

A place I haven't been to in more than fifteen years.

My family's legacy.

I glance around at what I can see of the property from the road and instantly notice the changes. Even from the outside looking in, I can see the updates and expansions done since the last time I stepped foot on the property. A brand new, larger pay hut and concession stand area, seating areas, and the old barn off to the right has been reroofed, the old wood plank siding given a facelift.

I spot movement near the barn and instantly recognize my cousin, Klint. Even though I haven't seen him since I was fourteen, I'd recognize him anywhere. We're built the same, with matching brown eyes. When we were growing up together, everyone mistook us for brothers instead of cousins.

We've kept in contact over the years, thanks to him tracking me down on social media, but this'll be the first time we've been face-to-face since that summer before my freshman year of high school. Since my dad and grandpa got into one hell of an argument, and we ended up moving away.

I haven't seen most of my extended family since.

As if sensing he's being watched, Klint stops what he's doing and glances toward the road. We stare at each other for a few moments, too far away to really catch facial expressions, but when he lifts his arm to wave, I know he recognizes me. I press on the gas and head for the employee entrance about a quarter of a mile to the right, and within a minute, I'm pulling up beside the barn.

Before I even have one foot out of the rental vehicle, my cousin is there. "Holy shit, man. It's damn good to see you." He pulls me into a hug, both of us squeezing a little harder and a bit longer than normal.

"Good to see you too," I reply. As soon as we separate, I add, "Wish it were under better circumstances."

He nods in understanding and glances toward the barn. "Yeah, me too. But it looks like he's gonna be okay."

I lift my chin in understanding, trying to ignore the knot of emotion firmly lodged in my throat. "I'm glad."

"Yeah, so...you ready for this?" he asks, a knowing grin on his face.

"As I'll ever be," I assure him, clapping my hands and rubbing my palms together. "Damn, I forgot how cold it is here."

Klint laughs. "Yeah, you're gonna have to grow some thick skin pretty quickly, man. Winter in Colorado is probably a lot different than winter in South Carolina."

I let out a snort of a laugh. "You're telling me. I remember that first winter we spent there. I was amazed when it didn't snow a single day all winter."

"I can't imagine," he retorts, glancing around at the fresh white snow blanketing the farm. Turning to me, he says, "I'm glad you're here."

"Me too." And not just because I'm helping my cousin and uncle while my grandpa is laid up in the hospital, recuperating from a stroke, but because this feels like a homecoming. Like a piece of my life has always been missing, and it's finally clicking into place. Wild how right it feels to be here, even after less than five minutes.

"Come on, let's head into the barn and I can give you the rundown."

I nod and follow, grabbing the thick winter work coat I had to purchase before arriving in Colorado from my rental. "This place looks great. You've all done a lot of work."

"We have," he confirms, walking to where the horses are and adding bales of alfalfa hay to their stalls. "The barn got a facelift about six years ago, and the new pay hut and concession area four years ago."

"It looks great, man, really."

"Thanks," he replies, stepping out of the final stall and leaning against the wall.

"Everyone is okay with me being here, right?" I finally address the elephant in the room.

Klint gives me a sad look. "Of course they are, B. We both know that shit that happened wasn't about you. Or me. But we were caught in the middle."

I nod and glance down at the dirt floor. "I shouldn't have stayed away." The guilt of walking away with my family almost fifteen years ago and never returning eats at me.

"Well, you're here now," Klint says, reaching over and slapping me on the back. "Gram is practically shooting rainbows and snowflake glitter out of her ass right now."

I bark out a laugh and shake my head. "That's an image."

He just grins. "She's going to visit Gramps this morning, but she'll be here this afternoon for a bit."

I nod, eager, yet a little nervous to see my grandma for the first time since my high school graduation. She flew out and attended the event, and I've remained in contact with her since, but not nearly as often as I should. That's on me.

"You'll get to meet my wife, Gretchen, and son, Noah, this weekend. She's still nursing a tweaked knee, thanks to slipping on some ice, but she'll for sure be here tomorrow and Sunday to work the pay hut."

"Can't wait," I tell him. I've kept up with Klint and his family, as well as my youngest cousin, Tasha, thanks to social media. Klint is two years younger than my twenty-nine years, and his wife is just a bit younger than him. They share a five-year-old son, who is the spitting image of his dad and loves to work beside him at the tree farm.

"Tasha gets out of class early today, so she'll be able to man the hut after two. Before then, we just make sure someone is always nearby. Plus, we have some part-time high schoolers who take care of the concession stand, so we don't have to worry about that part."

I nod in understanding.

"Dad will be here any minute, and so will Ray Campbell, our other employee."

My ears perk up at the name. "Ray Campbell? Really?"

He lifts his chin. "Yep. He's worked here for probably eleven or twelve years. Helps out year-round with the trees, pumpkins, greenhouses, and mowing. Gramps loves him."

Of course he does. Ray is a great guy. I grew up watching him work his ass off, raising his family, and giving his all.

But it's not just Ray I think about when I pull up memories from my first fourteen years of life. It's his youngest daughter, Joy. She was one of my best friends for several years, right up until we left town. In fact, we tried to remain in contact for a while, vowing to send weekly pen pal letters that would keep us in communication forever. Unfortunately, life happened, and those weekly letters slowly started to grow further and further apart until they stopped completely. Life in high school, with friends and sports, became too much for our young fourteen-year-old selves to maintain, and our friendship eventually died out.

That doesn't mean I haven't thought about her over the years. When major life events happened in high school, I'd wonder what she was doing. What sports did she play? Who asked her to prom? Did she earn valedictorian the way I assumed she did, since she was the smartest girl in the whole school?

Is she married now with kids?

I try not to think about that one, because as it turns out, I don't like that image, even though she was never mine to have. She was my friend, plain and simple. I never pictured her in any other way than a comrade, friend, buddy.

But lately, I can't help but wonder what happened to the pretty girl I once knew with vivid green eyes, dirty-blond hair, and a sprinkle of freckles over her nose.

"Glad to hear he's still around," I reply casually.

"Yep, for sure." Klint checks his watch. "He should be here in about thirty minutes."

"His wife good?"

"Oh, yeah. Cindy still cuts hair at the salon downtown, and their oldest, Eve, works there too. She's dating John Mitchell now, who is Noah's hero."

My eyebrows pull together in confusion.

"John's a paramedic and took care of Noah in the ER last winter when he came down with pneumonia. As far as my son thinks, John is the greatest guy in the world," he replies with a grin.

I remember John. He was two years older than me in school, but he always seemed like a solid guy, who treated all kids with kindness.

"And Joy?" I ask aloud, my heart starting to pick up a little after saying her name.

"Owns the bakery next door to the salon."

You couldn't scrape the smile off my face with a putty knife. Of course she runs a bakery. That girl was always obsessed with making anything and everything she could. First in an Easy-Bake Oven, and then, as soon as her mom would let her use the stove unsupervised, she really started to create masterpieces. Even at such a young age, I remember her always setting aside a little time to bake.

Before I can say anything or ask any more questions, the barn door opens, and my uncle walks in. His eyes immediately seek me out, as a smile spreads across his lips. "Burk."

"Hey, Uncle Karl," I reply, meeting him halfway and giving him a big hug.

"Look at you," he says, stepping back and taking me in from head to toe. I'm a couple of inches taller than he is, and his dark hair is grayer than it was the last time I saw him. His skin is weathered and aged, but he still looks exactly as I remember him from fifteen years ago. "How have you been?"

"Been good, thanks. You guys have done a lot with this place. It looks great," I tell him, earning me a smile full of pride.

He nods and looks around before returning his gaze to me. "Glad to have you here to help."

Again, my throat becomes dry. "More than happy to help, Uncle Karl. I'm glad you guys called," I state, taking a quick look toward Klint, who's the one who called to tell me about Grandpa's stroke and to ask if there was any way I could come help at the farm for the next month.

There was only one answer I could give.

Even though our family hasn't been that close the last fifteen or so years, I'd drop anything to help while Gramps recuperates.

It wasn't easy making it happen though. I had two furniture pieces I was commissioned to make before Christmas, and I had to call both clients and tell them I couldn't do them anymore. When I explained why, both were super cool and decided to keep the orders in place. We just pushed the production back to January and I offered a discount off their total price as a thank you.

"You sure you don't mind staying with Mom?" Karl asks, referring to my grandma. "You're more than welcome to have Klint's old room out at our place."

I wave off his comments. "I'm happy to stay with Gram. This way, I can help her with whatever she needs while she's with Gramps."

I was told it's going to be a couple of weeks before he's able to come home. While the stroke was considered mild, he has a lot of weakness on his left side and will need to go to a rehab center for a couple weeks to rebuild his strength. The goal is to have him home in plenty of time for Christmas, even though he won't be able to work his farm for a while.

Karl grins. "She's super excited to have you. You get the whole upstairs to yourself, since we moved them down to the first floor after her knee surgery two summers ago."

Just one more thing I've missed since moving away.

The barn door opens once more and in walks another blast from the past. "Rumor has it we have a new employee starting today to haze."

I bark out a laugh, my feet already carrying me toward Ray. "I don't think you can haze people anymore," I tell him, throwing my arms around his shoulders and giving him a hug.

"We keep our secrets around here," he teases. His comment makes me laugh even harder, since Snowflake Falls was never known for keeping secrets.

"Sure, sure," I reply, taking a good look at the man I remember from my childhood. "How are you?"

"I'm doing very well, thanks. Happy to see you here, despite the circumstances."

I nod in reply. "Glad I could come help out. It's been too long."

He's watching me closely. "It has. Everyone is going to be so happy to see you."

I can't help but wonder if he's including his youngest daughter in that group.

Before I can ask any more questions, my uncle speaks up, "Well, we're opening in thirty minutes. I don't think we'll be too busy today, but tomorrow and Sunday should be our biggest weekend of the year. It'll take all four of us cutting and wrapping trees. We do close at five tomorrow instead of six, since it's the big opening night of the festival."

My heart jumps in my chest as I think about the Snowflake Falls Family Festival. Every weekend from now through the end of the year, it's nothing but fun for the holidays, all outside, weather permitting. I remember spending every free minute I could during the month of December in the downtown square. Carnival games, amusement rides, ice skating, Christmas movies, food and cocoa. When I was asked to come home and help, attending the festival was one of the first things I thought about.

Of course, I might be too busy to even attend the festival. I am here to work, and make sure my family's farm is taken care of. Ensuring Gram has what she needs, whether at the hospital or here at home, is my top priority. Everything else comes in second, and that includes reconnecting with old friends.

"All right, let's get ready to go. Burk, you can shadow Klint today, but both Ray and I will be around too. If you have any questions, just holler," Uncle Karl says.

"Sounds good," I easily agree, ready to get to work.

"Let's take a quick ride around the property. I'll show you what sections we have open for tree cutting and where we keep all the supplies," Klint states.

I follow to an awaiting UTV with an all-weather cab enclosure, complete with doors and a windshield. "Well, this is a hell of a lot warmer than the old tractor we used to drive around back when we were kids," I state, climbing into the passenger seat.

Klint chuckles and starts up the machine. "Oh, we still have the tractor, and I'm sure you'll get a chance to drive it. Gramps still insists on using it, though in the last couple of years, he's gotten better about taking this. I think his blood is finally starting to thin a little in his old age."

I don't comment, especially because of the reason I'm here. Gramps is proving to be human after all, which to me is still a little crazy. He was always larger than life and the hardest worker I knew. When we left all those years ago, I didn't want to go. I begged my dad to let me stay at the farm, but he wouldn't hear it. Living in Colorado wasn't what he wanted, but he did it to please his father. Eventually, he couldn't do it anymore, and that's when the argument ensued. We ended up moving away, never to return.

I take a big chunk of that responsibility now, looking back. Maybe not while I was still a minor, but after graduating high school and becoming an adult, I should have visited. But I was young, dumb, and stupid. I had friends in South Carolina and a life there, and visiting my family back west didn't seem as important at the time.

Now, I'm righting that wrong.

Thankfully, Gramps is gonna recover from his stroke, but even then, I'm gonna stay in contact with my family and do my part. No more out of sight, out of mind. Especially around the holidays.

We spend about thirty minutes touring the farm. It hasn't changed much in the last fifteen years. Sure, the tree sections are different, but everything else has remained the same. Even the old houses look similar, despite some updating over that time.

There are three houses on the property. Gram and Gramp's house is the large one near the front of the farm, while there are two smaller ones tucked in the back corners of their land. Karl's house on one side and the one I grew up in on the other. Now, Klint and his family live there, and he promised to give me a tour of it one of these evenings.

We return to the front just after Ray opens the gate. Cars are already arriving, patrons ready to cut down their Christmas trees and start making holiday memories, and a wave of excitement rushes through me.

I get to be a part of that.

Klint parks the UTV beside the barn and grins. "Let's get to work.

Chapter Three

Joy

"We're almost out of the eggnog muffins," Jan hollers from the front of the bakery.

"On it," I reply, grabbing the third pan of delicious muffins I've made this morning.

Saturdays are usually my busiest day of the week, and today is no different, thanks to the kickoff of the festival. Most of the activities won't start until later, but nothing brings the people out like the first Saturday of December. They're hitting the tree farm, grabbing some new decorations, and even some sweet treats and coffees, all before heading out to the opening night of the festival later this evening, where one young lady will be crowned Miss Snowflake Falls.

I remember that competition. I participated my senior year of high school but fell just short of the title. I was named first runner-up and was completely devastated. My mom was the first title recipient thirty-six years ago, and my sister two years prior to me competing. But I didn't quite have what they did, and one of my classmates bested me that night. She deserved the crown, don't get me wrong. Tabbi Smythe made an incredible Miss Snowflake Falls that year, but I really would have liked to have won.

Yet even coming in second didn't dampen the sparkle of the entire night. From the welcome address from the mayor to the naming of the winner, I love sitting in my lawn chair, curled up in a warm blanket, and sipping a cup of hot cocoa. Not to mention being surrounded by snow-covered twinkle lights and the nostalgia of festivals past. There's nothing like it.

Tonight, The Sweet Escape will be open for an extended two-hour period prior to the start of the pageant. We will offer a very limited menu as to not compete with the other organizations selling food and drinks. The hot cocoa stand is always manned by a different organization or group, and at the end of the night, they keep whatever profits were made. Since that's a big part of their fundraising, I never sell hot cocoa from my bakery, opting for other Christmassy drinks to help keep you warm.

"This is the last of them," I tell Jan, sliding the tray of eggnog muffins into the display case and noting we're low on apple fritters too. "Let me grab what's left of the fritters, and I'll help."

I retrieve the other tray of fresh baked goods and slip them inside the case too. Considering it's still midmorning, I realize I might be in trouble where pastries are concerned. As soon as I can get to the kitchen to prep more, the better off I'll be.

After quickly washing my hands, I turn my attention to the counter and take the order of the next person in line. "What can I get you?" I ask with a warm smile.

"I'd like a vanilla raspberry latte and an eggnog muffin, please," the first of three women here together orders.

"I'll make drinks. You pull pastries and checkout," Jan says. This system will allow us to move through customers quicker, and we're not stepping on each other while doing it.

We work in unison to serve all three ladies as quickly as possible. I love watching their faces light up as I place their fresh baked good in front of them. They're chatting about going shopping after their breakfast break, so I make sure to tell them to visit Mom's salon next door after they're done here. She's open until one today, and they're offering a sale on certain products, as well as door prizes.

"We'll be sure to do that," the third lady replies, picking up her pastry and coffee before moving away from the counter to join her friends at one of the tables.

"How can I help you?" I ask the next person in line as he steps up to the counter.

"What's good here, Easy-Bake?"

The nickname causes me to pause as my brain is peppered with flashbacks. I glance up into smiling brown eyes that look so familiar, yet so very different. His face has aged considerably, since the last time I saw him he was fourteen.

"Holy shit! Burkey Turkey?" I whisper, my jaw dropping as I stare at the man at the counter. He's no longer the tall, skinny kid I remember from my childhood. Oh, no. Burk Whitman is all man now, from his rugged, gorgeous face to his scruffy jaw. He's still tall with a lean frame, but his physique is much more filled out than before. He's muscular without being overly so, if that makes sense.

He makes a face, reminding me of a time when I was a kid and first gave him that nickname. Our third grade class put on a Thanksgiving play for the school, and Burk won the role of the turkey. I've never let him live it down, always using the nickname he hated so much. "You know I hate that nickname," he grumbles. "Klint told me you owned this place, and I just had to come see for myself," he adds with a big smile that seems to light up his entire face.

Holy crap, Burk Whitman is h-o-t, hot!

My feet are moving before I can even reconsider. I'm around the counter and throwing my arms around him in a fierce hug. He returns the gesture, and it's right in this moment I catch a whiff of his clean, woodsy scent. It sends a shiver through my body and does something to my lady bits that's unexpected. I feel my nipples pebble beneath my sweater and a rush of moisture between my legs.

All from soap...

Well, Jingle Bells, he freaking smells amazing too!

"I can't believe you're here," I state, grinning from ear to ear and trying not to think about exactly how hard his body felt when I hugged him.

But then it hits me as to *why* he's likely here, and I quickly sober.

"Yeah, me either," he says softly, his soulful dark eyes locked on mine. It causes my heart to skip a beat and my breathing to quicken. "Listen, I know you're busy. Hell, I'm heading back out to the farm for work. But I wanted to drop by and say hello. Plus, my stomach's growling and whatever you have in that case smells delicious," he adds with a grin and a wink.

"Well, do I have a treat for you, my old friend," I tease, returning to behind the counter and offering a quick apology to those lined up behind him. "What can I get you to drink?" I ask, while pulling both an eggnog muffin and an apple fritter from the case and slipping them inside a white paper bag.

"Regular coffee, with extra sugar and cream, please," he says, making me grin once more. Burk always liked the sweets when we were growing up, so it doesn't surprise me he adds plenty to his coffee.

"Here," Jan says, handing over the drink.

"How much?" Burk asks, pulling some bills from his wallet.

"Your money's no good here, Burkey Turkey," I insist with a wink.

He huffs out a deep breath and shakes his head, turning to his right and slipping the cash inside the tip jar. "You can't make money if you don't charge, Easy-Bake."

"Yeah, well, that's for me to worry about."

Burk reaches for the bag and coffee but hesitates to leave. There's a line of customers behind him, but all I want to do is stand here and talk to my old friend some more. "Maybe I'll see you around and we can catch up?"

"I'd love that," I reply. "If you come to the pageant tonight, stop by and see us."

He nods, taking a step to his right to allow the next customer to approach the counter. "You still sit by the big oak tree?"

"You know it," I reply, again with a grin. I can't seem to stop smiling.

He nods. "I'll see what time I get done at the farm, but I'm serious about catching up, Easy-Bake."

"Me too, Burkey Turkey." I can't believe how easily we fall into an old, familiar banter, even though it's been fifteen years.

He lifts his chin and adds, "Talk to you soon."

"Have a good day," I reply, shamelessly watching as he walks toward the front entrance. He's wearing work boots, jeans, a thick winter coat, and a stocking cap on his head, but I can still see the niceness of his ass through the worn denim. He pushes out the door and walks past the front window.

"Girl," Jan sings just over my left shoulder. "That boy is f-i-n-e, fine, and his eyes were all over you."

A blush creeps up my neck, as I do everything I can to brush off her comment. "Please," I reply with a tsk. "He's practically my oldest friend. I haven't seen him since the summer before our freshman year of high school."

"Mmhmm, keep telling yourself that."

I roll my eyes and give every bit of attention I can to my customers. They keep us hopping and we're busier than expected on a Saturday morning, but I wouldn't want it any other way. Seeing people enjoy my pastries is the highlight of my life. It'll never get old, even when I'm exhausted and my feet hurt from standing for fourteen hours a day. The satisfaction I feel makes every early morning and late night worth it.

"Do you want me to come back later?" Jan asks when the morning rush finally dies down.

"No, Krista and I have it covered. It's easy when you're only offering two snack and two drink options," I tell my faithful employee. Jan has worked for me since I opened four years ago and doesn't mind working five days a week. She also doesn't require medical insurance, since her husband carries it, so that's a plus for me. Insurance is expensive enough when you're self-employed, which is why I carry the bare minimum on myself.

Krista helps me during these types of special events, where I'm only open a few hours and have a very select menu. She's been doing it since I opened, and I'm so grateful for my closest friend. She does it for free, insisting she be paid in pastries and coffee.

"Well, I'll be around if you get swamped and need help," she informs me, hanging her apron on a hook in the kitchen and clocking out.

It's just after one and she's off for the day. My regular business hours are six to two, but I often host pop-up events, especially during the holidays. Plus, since I live right upstairs, it's easy to make arrangements with customers for pick-up orders. After work is the most popular time for meeting a customer, and fortunately, I'm super close.

"Thanks, Jan. Enjoy the festival kickoff tonight," I reply as she makes her way to the back entrance.

"You too!"

When I'm bathed in silence, my mind instantly returns to thinking about Burk. I can't believe he's here, back in Snowflake Falls. I remember the night he came to me and said he was leaving, that his dad and grandpa got into a huge fight. Within two short weeks, their entire lives were packed up into a large U-Haul, and they were headed for the East Coast.

Those first few weeks, Burk hated it. It was hot, a different type of heat than what we have in Colorado. Plus, he didn't know anyone and would complain as such. We kept in contact the old-fashioned way, with letters. But we also sent texts and emails.

However, when school began shortly after his arrival in South Carolina, he started making friends, he joined the basketball team, and even a few clubs. Slowly, over the next few months, the letters started to get fewer and fewer. The texts practically stopped and there were no more emails. Our friendship...moved on.

For me too. I started high school. I had always been friends with Krista, but we became inseparable. We both played volleyball and joined the FFA, and suddenly, our lives were changing. Evolving. I do remember the last time I had texted him though. It was that following Christmas, and I received an online subscription to a baking platform from my parents. All my friends were asking for designer clothes or the latest name in athletic shoes. But not me. I wanted this online subscription that had articles, videos, and interviews with the biggest bakers in the world. Not to mention, recipes. I was so thrilled, the first person I wanted to tell was Burk.

He replied right away, super excited on my behalf. He knew what this gift meant to me, probably because I talked about it all year. It wasn't even that expensive of a gift, but it still held more value than anything else I could have possibly received, and I was thrilled to receive it.

But that was the last time I texted him, and he in return. Our lives were consumed with school, friends, and everything you'd imagine two fourteen-year-olds did. I played in the snow. He went on trips to the beach with friends. We changed, and so did the landscape of our friendship.

Have I thought about him over the years? Of course I have. Many times. Every year when I'd go to the tree farm to pick my tree for that season, I'd picture two little kids running and playing through the rows of evergreens. I'd see us sitting at a picnic table, eating an apple donut and enjoying hot cocoa. I'd see him surrounded by family, the same people who still run the tree farm to this day.

As far as I know, Burk and his parents never returned to Snowflake Falls. I heard his grandma went out for his high school graduation, something she shared with my mom while at a hair appointment right before she left for the trip. I wanted to send a message for Burk with her, but by the time I was told she was going, she was already off to South Carolina.

His grandpa didn't go. There were harsh words said by both father and son that fateful day fifteen years ago, but I was told he sent his love to his oldest grandson. I've always wondered how deep that wedge had to be driven for family to walk away the way Burk's father and mother did. Personally, I can't imagine not seeing or speaking to my parents almost daily, and I could never envision living any other place than right here in Snowflake Falls.

And I've never witnessed that side of Dale Whitman either. He's always been nothing short of kind and gentle, even when he was working long, hard days at the farm. He very much reminds me of my own grandpa, who passed away when I was twenty-three. I don't remember my mom's dad, who passed when I was just a couple years old.

I spend the afternoon preparing sweet treats for tonight's pop-up opening. Krista and I will be selling gingerbread cookies and Christmas cake pops from five to six forty-five, or until sold out. I'm also limiting our drink menu to a hot gingerbread latte or a decadent raspberry and dark chocolate mocha, since hot cocoa and coffee is available at the main stand near the park entrance.

Our downtown is a square, with a city block-sized park smack dab in the middle, complete with playground, pavilion, and gazebo. My favorite part, however, is the ice-skating rink. I spend random winter nights there often, mostly because it's directly across the street. During the week, it's not nearly as used. There are even times I have to clean the freshly fallen snow off the ice to skate. The city employees take great care of it, but when snow falls as often as it does here, they can't always keep up with it.

At four thirty, the back door opens and in walks Krista. "Hello," she hollers, wearing a festive sweater and dark jeans.

"Hey," I reply, starting to take today's offerings to the front display case.

"I think it might snow," she says, slipping off her coat, gloves, and stocking cap and hanging them on the hook by the back door.

"I love when it snows during the pageant," I confess, secretly hoping to see the flakes fly before the end of the night.

Our pageant isn't quite like others. It's pretty short, all things considered, and there aren't nearly as many categories as most pageants. An introduction portion, talent, and then evening gown, which always includes layers for warmth and usually a fuzzy shawl or jacket.

"You would," she retorts, jumping right in to carry the trays to the front. "What are we serving tonight?"

"Christmas cake pops. They're chocolate cake pops with a white chocolate coating and festive sprinkles, and gingerbread cookies with royal icing."

"Mmm," she practically sings as we load up the case.

As we prepare to open the doors, I say, "Uhh, do you remember Burk Whitman?"

Krista whips around. "Of course I do. I remember when he moved away right before we went to high school. Why?"

I swallow over the dryness in my throat. "He came in today."

"What? Really?"

I shrug. "He's here helping his family, since Dale Whitman is out for the season from his stroke."

"You two were really good friends when you were younger."

"Yeah, we were, but we haven't really talked for, like, fifteen years," I say, making sure we're ready to make our two specialty drinks.

"Huh," she starts, reading over the recipe cards for both drinks. Turning my way, she asks, "Is he cute?"

My heart rate jumps at the thought. "I...I mean, he's all right."

My best friend gasps. "Oh my God, you think he's cute!"

"I do not," I retort, a little too forcefully. I practically have guilty written across my forehead.

"You so do, don't deny it. I know you better than anyone, and you're blushing right now and refusing to look at me."

I turn and meet her gaze, trying to keep my true feelings hidden, but it's no use. She sees right through me. "Fine, he's cute."

"I knew it! What if you two fall in love, get married, and live happily ever after?" my best friend bellows, practically bouncing on her toes with giddy excitement.

"Stop right now! It's not like that. I probably won't even see him. He's here working, Krista. He'll be so busy at the tree farm, I bet I've seen the last of him during his time here," I state, trying to convince her as much as I try to convince myself.

She grins widely and shakes her head. "We'll see about that."

Chapter Four

Burk

With my hands shoved in the pockets of my coat, I slowly make my way toward the downtown square. There are people everywhere, up and down the sidewalks and snow-covered park. The entire place is lit up with white Christmas lights, while holiday music is piped through speakers throughout the area.

I wait with about a dozen other townspeople for the crosswalk signal to change, granting us permission to move to the other side of the street. As soon as it changes, we all start to walk. When we reach the other side, most head to what I assume is the hot cocoa stand. That's where it always was when I was growing up and attending this festival, and that was usually our first stop too.

I head in the opposite direction though, just so I don't get too caught up in the masses. Walking toward the pavilion where the pageant will be held, I take in the faces around me. Some look vaguely familiar, but many I don't recognize at all. It causes another wave of sadness to wash through me.

Today, at work, I reconnected with a few people I knew from my time here. Mrs. Englewood, my old third grade teacher, and her husband came out to get a tree. It was nice catching up with them for a bit while we searched for their perfect tree and I cut it down. It was weird taking their offered tip after I loaded it up into their pickup truck, but no amount of refusing would deter them. I took their ten-dollar tip and shoved it in my pocket before sending them on their way.

The carnival rides won't run until tomorrow night, as to not take away from the main stage entertainment: the pageant. I remember riding those things for hours and hours, from the moment they opened until the last spin they took at the end of the night. Joy was always there with her sister, enjoying the rides all weekend long.

I spot the ice-skating rink too, and again, my thoughts are consumed with memories of Joy. If she wasn't on the rides, she was skating. I went with her often, but I was never as good as she was. It was amazing I could stay standing and continually moving in the same circle as the rest of the skaters. I was athletic, sure, but there's definitely an art to ice skating.

My eyes move toward the bakery, all on their own, and I'm surprised to see it lit up. In fact, there appears to be a line out the door, so that's where I head. While everyone else is grabbing their sweet treats and drinks from the stand manned by the local church youth group, I walk to where Joy is, a little too much spring in my step.

I can't help it. Adult Joy is fucking gorgeous.

She definitely grew up in all the right places. Her hips are a little curvy and her tits the perfect handful. At least for my hands.

I should most certainly *not* be thinking about her this way, but I'm human. And a guy. And she's checking some of my boxes where females are concerned. Maybe it's the fact I haven't dated much in recent years. My last girlfriend was Sharon, who was practically picking out wedding china by our second month together. She would text me ads for rings and venues, and I had to have the awkward conversation that I just wasn't ready for that. She swore she wasn't either but loved to browse for "someday." Yet proved me wrong when I got a call from a minister of a church, who informed me he had a date open up three weeks from that day and asked if I'd like to book it.

Fuck. No.

She didn't make it easy to break up either. She insisted I was overreacting, that she wasn't actively planning the nuptials I wasn't ready for, and for weeks, would show up at my workshop and house unannounced and uninvited. Once, when my friend Drew was over, she barged in, accusing me of cheating on her. The only thing she managed to do was interrupt the basketball game we were watching and have a restraining order slapped against her.

Turns out, it wasn't her first.

I was a bit more hesitant over who I started talking to in a bar after that. Who would blame me?

Not all the women from my past were like Sharon, however. I dated a girl for almost two years in my early twenties, and things were really great. I thought she might be the one. We had a lot in common, and she didn't mind if I'd lock myself in my workshop for hours on end and barely come out to sleep or eat. But at the end of the day, there was one major difference we couldn't quite get on the same page about.

I wanted kids eventually, but she did not.

Last I heard, she was happily married with four dogs and a cat.

When I reach The Sweet Escape, the line is just inside the door, and even though I'm pretty sure I recognize the woman in front of me as the owner of the small grocery store here in town, I don't say anything. Instead, I watch the woman behind the counter as she rings up the customer at the front of the line.

Joy laughs and smiles, seems genuinely happy to serve each and every customer who approaches the counter. I recognize Krista behind her, mostly from the fiery red hair. You can tell they've worked together plenty in the past and have a routine. Krista works on making drinks, while Joy grabs the treats and works the register.

As I approach the front of the line, I notice the signage about the limited menu. She's offering two drink options and two treats, and I'm sure that's for simplicity purposes and to not compete with the hot cocoa stand in the square.

When the couple in front of me reaches the counter, that's when Joy notices me over their shoulders. She hesitates for a brief second but then smiles as she turns her attention to the payment system. I follow her every move as she hollers out the drink orders to Krista and then retrieves two cake pops from the display. She steals glances my way as she completes her task, and just as I take a step up to the counter, Krista turns around, her eyes widening with surprise.

"Holy crap, Burk?" she squeals, running around the counter and giving me a huge hug.

"Hey, Krista. How are you?" I ask, returning the gesture.

"I'm great, thanks." She gives me a quick once-over and hits me square in the middle of the chest. "Dang, you grew up well, Mr. Whitman."

I snort a laugh. "Well, thank you, ma'am." I pretend to tip my hat.

Krista looks over her shoulder and grins widely at her friend. "Hmm, look who's here, Joy. It's *Burk*." She draws out my name, enunciating it and popping the K.

Joy narrows her eyes at her friend and blushes. Something tells me there's an inside joke I'm not privy to. "I see him," Joy replies with a deadpan voice.

Krista hits me on the arm playfully. "What can we get you?"

I glance over at the menu for tonight and request, "Well, I've never been a huge fan of gingerbread—"

"But you've never had Joy's gingerbread," Krista states, moving behind the counter once more and starting to make a drink.

"If you want the other drink, that's fine. Don't let her bully you into something you don't want," Joy says, embarrassment lighting her face.

"Well, Krista cut me off, but I was about to say practically the same thing. I'll have a gingerbread latte and one of the cake pops, please." I pull cash from my wallet, and thankfully, this time, she quickly rings it up.

"Seven dollars, please."

As she grabs one of the cake pops and slips it inside a small bag, I pull a ten out and set it on the counter.

"What are your plans for this evening, Burk?" Krista asks, finishing up my warm drink.

"I thought I'd try to catch some of the pageant," I tell her.

"Us too! Joy closes at six forty-five so we can join her family under the big oak tree. You should come too!" Krista states, the glint in her eyes letting me know she's up to something.

I flash her an easy smile. "I don't want to interrupt family time."

"You're not!" Krista declares, completely ignoring her best friend.

Joy looks a little mortified, and I can't help but feel like an imposition. "We'll see," I finally state, hoping to appease both women without making anyone uncomfortable. Just because Joy mentioned us catching up doesn't mean she wants to do it tonight.

The air feels thick as I take my change from Joy and slip it into the tip jar. There's a line a mile long behind me, and it's nearing her closing time. She doesn't have time to entertain me, so I step to the side to wait for my drink and the next customer can place their order.

I keep my eyes down as I wait, and fortunately, it only takes another minute before my drink is ready. "Here ya go, Burk," Krista says eagerly, sliding the cup across the counter. "Come by the tree, all right?"

I nod, grabbing my drink and lifting it in a salute. Just as I start to turn, I see Joy watching me. "Thanks," I state, hoping not to cause her any more discomfort.

Heading for the door, I still feel her eyes on me, but I don't look back. She was clearly embarrassed that her friend invited me to join her and her family for the pageant. Because she doesn't want to hang out? Maybe she's dating someone? Who knows, but I'm not going to make this awkward for everyone.

I make my way around to the opposite side of the park and watch as the pageant gets ready to begin. Holiday music is playing, and everyone seems to be grabbing their final refreshments before the competition starts. I notice the lights in the bakery turn off as a handful of people exit the storefront.

Taking my cake pop out of the small bag, I steal a bite of the chocolate cake on a stick. The flavors explode on my tongue, and all I can think about is how it's so much better than any basic chocolate treat. Then I sample the gingerbread latte, and I can't get over how damn good it is. I don't even like gingerbread, but I'd purchase another one of these drinks tomorrow if she offered them.

"Burk?"

Looking toward the voice, I smile when I see Joy's older sister, Eve. "Hey, Even Steven," I say with a chuckle.

She hits me in the chest and pulls me into a hug, careful not to spill my drink or knock the cake pop from my hand. "I see you've been to the bakery," she states, noting the logo printed on the side of the cup.

"Just left there." I look over at the man standing beside Eve and shift my cup to my other hand so I can extend it. "John Mitchell, right?"

He nods, taking my hand and giving it a shake. "Yep. Nice to see you again, Burk."

"It's been a while," I confirm, even though neither need it.

"How's your grandpa?" Eve asks, her green eyes full of concern.

"He's doing much better. Hoping to transfer him to the rehab center in a few days so he can start working on getting stronger to come home."

"Oh, good." The music starts to get a little louder, drawing everyone's attention to the stage. "Did you bring a chair? You can come sit with us."

When I told Gram I was coming to the pageant, she told me to grab one of the bag chairs out of the garage, but I didn't know if I was staying long, so I didn't. But I also don't want to make Joy any more uncomfortable than I clearly did earlier. "I'm just here for a few minutes. Gotta work early tomorrow," I tell her with a chuckle.

"Aww, well, if you change your mind, we're over by the tree. You're welcome to come sit with us."

"I appreciate it," I tell her as the stage lights brighten and everyone around us turns their attention to the mayor, who is about to do the customary welcome and officially kick off the festival.

"I'm sure we'll see you around," John says, reaching for Eve's hand. "We plan to come out and pick out our tree tomorrow."

"I'll be there."

With waves, they take off toward their spot in the crowd, and I'm left standing in the back, off to the side, out of the way. I listen as the mayor finishes his welcome and the master of ceremonies joins him on the stage. Margaret Hamilton has served as the emcee of the pageant since the very beginning. I'm not sure how old that makes her, but she still moves well and sounds exactly the same. The only difference is a slight limp with her left leg and her blond hair turned gray.

Four contestants start the competition while I finish off my cake pop. A few people still mill around the sidewalks, and my eyes are constantly scanning. I recognize a few people but have no clue who most are, especially the kids.

Movement catches my attention, and I immediately recognize the woman heading my way. Joy's wearing a thick winter coat with some sort of faux-fur around the hood, a stocking cap with reindeer on it, and boots that look like she's ready to hike the snow-covered mountains. "Hi," she says with a shy grin.

"Hi," I reply, slipping the stick from my cake pop into the bag and placing it in my coat pocket to discard later.

"How was it?" she asks, lifting her chin toward the cup in my other hand.

"Delicious," I confirm, earning a gorgeous smile that lights up her green eyes.

"I'm glad you like it." After a few awkward seconds, she asks, "Are you just going to stand back here and watch the pageant?"

I shrug and glance at the stage. "I don't think I'm staying long."

After another few seconds she drops her gaze and says, "I'm, uh, sorry Krista was so pushy earlier."

"It's fine," I assure her.

"No, it's not. Sometimes she tries to play matchmaker for me, and it's really annoying. She got married two years ago and thinks I need to be just as deliriously happy as she is," she mutters, sticking out her tongue.

"Which part made you get all weird? The deliriously happy or the trying to set you up with me?" I ask in a teasing tone, even though I'm not sure I'm teasing at all.

Her eyes turn serious as she looks me up and down for a brief moment. She clears her throat and looks away as she mutters, "Not the latter."

A wave of excitement sweeps through me, and I can't stop myself from smiling. "Was it my boyish good looks or my strong, handsome jawline?"

She snorts a giggle that makes my balls tighten. "Handsome jawline, Burkey Turkey? Really?"

I shrug. "I've been told it's one of my best features."

Joy shakes her head as she laughs before sobering. Leaning in she whispers, "Huh, I would have guessed your ass would be considered your best feature."

All I can do is grin like a lunatic.

Clearing her throat, I catch a hint of a blush on her cheeks before she says, "Well, you might as well come over and sit with us for a bit. Come on, I have an extra chair."

My legs are moving before my brain can even process what's happening. "Do you want me to walk in front of you so you can check out my assets, Easy-Bake?" I tease, earning a giggle from the woman beside me.

"Smart-ass," she mutters as we start to make our way through the masses of townspeople sitting in the park, watching the pageant.

When we approach the tree, I spot two free chairs sitting beside the rest of her family, and a wave of delight hits me hard in the chest. She did bring me a seat. "Look who's here," Joy announces quietly when we reach the tree.

"Burk!" Cindy bellows, jumping up from her seat and giving me a warm hug. When she pulls back, she adds, "Ray has been talking about you being back nonstop. It's so good to see you."

"You as well, ma'am."

"Oh, just call me Cindy. Ma'am makes me feel old."

I chuckle. "You're definitely not old. You don't look a day over thirty-five."

She gently hits my shoulder and shakes her head. "You're my new favorite person."

I say a quick hello to Ray, Eve, John, and another woman who looks familiar. "Ariel Lehman," she greets, connecting the dots and throwing me a wave.

"Right, nice to see you again."

Joy takes one of the empty seats on the far side of the group, and I know if I want to skirt out of here, this is my opportunity. I could easily make a quick excuse and go back to my gram's house. There's no reason for me to have a seat and watch the pageant with the Campbell family.

"Have a seat, son. The competition just started," Ray states.

And that's what I do. Any thought of leaving vacates my mind instantly, and I take the final remaining seat beside Joy. We're close—right next to each other. I catch a whiff of something sweet, like cinnamon and sugar dusting her skin. It makes me harder than I've ever been before, and that's concerning.

Why?

She's my friend, plain and simple.

I'm not supposed to be fantasizing about licking her bare skin, even if the idea is appealing.

So, I'll sit here and not think about all the things I'd do to Joy Campbell if I had the chance.

Turns out, that's much easier said than done.

Chapter Five

Joy

I can feel his eyes on me, but as the pageant wraps up and the winner is announced, I do everything I can not to look his way. I'm afraid, if I do, he'll see how badly he affects me written all over my face. I most definitely can't look over at my sister. She'll know immediately and will latch on to that like a dog with a bone. So I sit tensely in my bag chair and watch the competition, recalling how excited and nervous I felt when I was up on that stage a little over ten years ago.

"I think we have a great princess this year," Mom says, always the diplomat. She says the same thing every year, even if the winner chose the other hair salon for her pageant hair.

"I agree," Eve states, grabbing their chairs and starting to slip them inside the bags.

I remain quiet as I reach for the blue bag that holds my chair, but before I can execute the task, Burk is reaching for my chair and sliding it inside the bag. He does the same to the one he was sitting in.

"Thank you," I tell him, my throat a little dry.

"Of course. Thanks for letting me sit with you guys."

"You're always welcome, son," Dad announces, clapping Burk on the back of the shoulder.

He nods and turns his attention to my sister and her boyfriend. "Eve and John, it was good to see you both again."

"You'll see us tomorrow for sure. We have to come pick out our tree," my sister states with enthusiasm. She turns to me. "You're coming too, right?"

I nod. "I'll meet you out there. I'm not walking and dragging that thing back to town on a sled."

Eve rolls her eyes at me. "Whatever. It's tradition."

"No, it's your tradition. Mine is to throw it in the back of Dad's truck."

When we were growing up, Dad and Mom would always walk us out to the tree farm to pick out our tree. We'd find the perfect one for our space, cut it down, and then drag it back to the house on a sled. We only lived a handful of blocks away from the farm, and thankfully, it sits on the edge of town. However, now I'm farther away. My apartment is in the middle of the downtown square, and that alone adds a good four blocks to the walk.

No thank you.

Dad usually delivers my tree, but since I'm anxious to get the one in my apartment put up tomorrow, I'm planning to borrow his truck and bring it to town.

"Do you want me to stop by and help you carry it up the stairs?" John offers.

"You guys will be busy with your own tree," I state, waving off his offer. "I'll be fine." Dragging the tree upstairs alone isn't ideal, but it's been done before. It usually just creates a bigger mess with the pine needles. Nothing a broom and dustpan can't handle.

"Still," he replies. "It'll only take a few minutes. I can run over when you get back with it."

Before I can tell John that's not necessary, I hear, "I can help."

I look Burk's way and shake my head. "You have to work though."

"I can take my lunch and help you," he assures, shocking me with his suggestion.

"I couldn't ask you to do that," I resist.

"You didn't. I offered." He flashes me a playful grin that's a strong mixture of the playful boy I remember and the gorgeous man standing before me today.

"Umm," I reply, feeling a little off-kilter.

"That's good of you, Burk. I'll make sure you get a lunch around the time Joy is there," Ray states, looking awfully pleased.

"Well, I need to get back to the bakery," I state, picking up my bag chair and slipping the carrying strap over my shoulder. I reach for the second one, the chair I brought in the off-chance Burk would be joining us, he refuses to hand it over.

"I'll carry it."

I roll my eyes and turn to my family. "I'll see you tomorrow."

Eve steps in and gives me a hug. "Want some help cleaning up?"

"No, I got it. Go home with your boyfriend to your kitties."

My sister flashes an easy smile. They still live separately, but I don't think for much longer. Their houses are beside each other's and they jump back and forth between the two, sleeping together every night. They even move their cats from one house to the other so Miss Snowflake and Biggie can be together. "If you're sure."

"I'm sure. Let me know when you're going to be there to pick out your tree."

She nods and reaches for John's hand. I watch as they take off together, so happy they found each other again after dating in high school.

"I'll see you tomorrow, sweetheart," Dad says, placing a kiss on my cheek.

"Night, Dad."

Mom gives me a wave. "Love you, Joy."

"Love you too," I tell her as she takes my dad's hand and walks toward the salon where their vehicle is parked.

I watch them go, smiling slightly at the sight of them together. They've always been a relationship goal for myself and my sister. Of course, when we were growing up, it was gross and a little annoying to see them so touchy feely and in love. Dad was always holding Mom's hand, kissing her hello and goodbye, and always being very attentive to her. Now, they're the epitome of relationship goals. I see what they have, and that's what I want someday.

Of course, I'm not gonna lie. I thought I'd have that by now. I turned twenty-nine at the end of October, and I definitely thought I'd be in a different place. Not as far as my business goes, but my personal life. I wanted to be married with a kid or two by this point, and that hasn't happened. In fact, not even close. I've dated, but no one stuck. Heck, no one has really blown my socks off with *the* kiss. You know the one that curls your toes and makes you forget your own name?

Has never happened.

I probably wouldn't even believe all the hype, but my sister Eve has told me all about it after she reconnected with John. She dated some loser who cheated on her before that, and there were definitely no toes curling there. But with John? She says it's pure magic. Like every day is Christmas, wrapped in snow-covered twinkle lights and a big red bow.

I want that.

"Ready?" Burk's voice breaks through my thoughts.

"Yep."

He walks with me as we make our way toward the bakery. My parents are far enough ahead they can't hear our conversation as I ask, "How's your grandpa doing?"

"Really good. I guess they got him up today. When Gram got there, he was sitting in the chair. She couldn't wait to tell us when she came back to the farm for a bit this afternoon."

I look from the left to the right, making sure no one is coming before we cross the street.

"A jaywalker, huh? I should have known you'd turn into a delinquent."

I bark out a laugh and start digging my keys out of my pocket. "I'm the furthest thing from a delinquent. The worst I've ever done is steal a piece of candy from the grocery store when I was eight. Mom made me march back in there, hand it over, and apologize."

"I remember. You were grounded for two weeks and couldn't come out and play."

"It was the worst! I wanted to play outside so bad," I whine, recalling how heartbroken I was when my friends were out playing at the park and riding their bikes together, while I was stuck in my room with no TV or phone. It was torture, and I definitely learned my lesson.

I go to the front entrance and release the lock. "Come on in," I state, holding the old glass with wood trim door wide enough for him to enter.

"Where should I put these?" he asks.

"We'll go put them by the back door. I'll take them upstairs when I go up for the night."

He gives me a strange look. "You live up there?"

"Yep," I reply, moving into the kitchen and turning on the light. "It's incredibly easy to get to work in the morning," I tease.

Burk gives me one of those panty-melting smiles that makes me shiver as it reaches its mark. "So, what all do you have to do yet?" he asks, taking in the space.

"I have to clean up from tonight's pop-up shop. Some dishes, sweeping, mopping, that kind of thing," I tell him, removing my coat, gloves, and hat and hanging them on a hook at the back door. He does the same as I move to the industrial double sink and start the water.

"I can help."

"You don't have to. I know you have to work tomorrow," I insist, adding the dish soap to the running water.

He shrugs his shoulders and looks around. "I've got time. Broom?"

I point to the closet on the back wall. "There."

He nods and retrieves the item, getting to work. Fortunately, it's not too bad, since I cleaned after I closed this afternoon and had most of the baking done. The only dishes are the trays I used in the display case and a few stirring spoons and cups left from the coffee drinks.

I try to ignore how easy and comfortable it feels to have him here. Chance, a former boyfriend I had for about six months, never offered to help me. Even if I was cleaning up at the end of a long day, he would take the free coffee drink and pastry I prepared and sit and watch me. Now, don't get me wrong—I don't expect anyone to help—but the occasional offer would be nice.

I start to clean the serving trays and whatnot, stacking them carefully in the drying rack. As I work, Burk says, "So, I have a question."

Glancing over my shoulder, I make eye contact with him and nod, indicating he can ask whatever it is he's curious about.

"Your mom and sister went up on stage during the Miss Snowflake Falls pageant as former princesses. You didn't want to compete?"

I rinse off the spatula, slip it onto the rack, and turn off the water. "I did. I came in second."

He stops his sweeping and levels me with a look. "What? How could you not win? You would have made a perfect princess. You're smart, talented, love Christmas. You're...beautiful."

Beautiful.

I feel the blush creep up my neck and avert my gaze for a moment while I try to collect my thoughts. "I was sad to lose, but the young woman who won deserved it. Do you remember Tabbi Smythe?"

"I do. She had dark hair and was friends with Lydia Johnston, who lives near the farm."

"Yes, that's her. To be honest, she made a great princess," I tell him, diving back into the dishes to finish the trays.

He's quiet for several seconds before breaking the silence. "You would have been better."

Dropping my chin to my chest, I smile at his sweet words. Clearing my throat, I ask, "So what have you been up to, Burkey Turkey?"

He chuckles at my use of his nickname and grabs the dustpan to sweep up what's on the floor. "I make furniture."

I spin around, water dripping from my hands. "You make furniture? Seriously?"

With a slight grin, he nods in confirmation. "Mostly tables, like coffee tables, end tables, nightstands, and kitchen or dining room tables, but also beds, chairs, and bookshelves."

"Wow, that's way cool, Burkey Turkey. Can I see some of your stuff sometime?"

"Sure," he replies with a shrug. "I have pictures on my phone."

Returning my attention to finishing the dishes, I ask, "So what got you into that?"

"Well, when we moved to South Carolina, our next-door neighbor had a woodworking shop out behind his house. I often found myself over there, asking questions about the tools and machinery he had and about the different types of wood. I spent all my free time over there, soaking up every ounce of knowledge he offered. I made everything from shelves to signs and eventually small tables. I loved it, so when I graduated, I worked a couple of years for a local construction company and saved money to start buying my own tools and machinery and started making things for local craft shows and whatnot. I made a name for myself and eventually was able to quit the construction job and just make furniture full time."

"Where do you sell your stuff?" I ask, completely enthralled.

"Mostly at a local furniture store there in town. I learned it was much easier to let them do the selling for me, so they purchase pieces at a slight discount and offer them in their store. It works out better for me because I don't have to worry about staging and space. They get first dibs, and if there's something they don't want, I post it online. I've had very good luck that way. I do special order commissioned pieces too, especially around the holidays."

I release the drain plug and rinse out the sink. Grabbing a towel, I turn and prop my hip against the stainless steel, giving him my full attention. "That's pretty badass, Burkey Turkey."

"Thanks," he replies, dumping what he's cleaned up off the floor into the trash can.

"What's your business called?" I have every intention of doing some online stalking later tonight.

He averts his gaze and blushes. Yes, blushes, like face on fire in full embarrassment mode blushing. "Uhh, it's called Joyful Furnishings."

My mouth drops open just a bit as I mull over his words. Is there some hidden meaning behind his business name? Do I *want* there to be a meaning? "That's a cool name," I mutter, my throat suddenly dry. What does this mean?

Burk flashes me an easy smile. "Thanks." He glances toward the front of the bakery. "Shall I go and sweep up there?"

"Sure," I reply, stealing a glance at his ass as he walks away. *Very nice ass.*

I wasn't kidding when I thought it was his best feature. His smile is a close second, but this ass? Could end wars in several countries.

Walking over to the speaker system, I flip it on and let the sounds of the season fill the space. I love this time of year for so many reasons, and one of them is the fact I can play holiday music until the end of the year. It's my absolute favorite, especially when they play some of the classics. Not that I don't like all the new versions of

Christmas music, but there's nothing like hearing Andy Williams, Bing Crosby, and Frank Sinatra belt out the classics.

Grabbing the sanitation solution, I clean the inside of the display case and then spray down the glass with window cleaner. As I work, I forget about Burk being here. I hum along to the music and occasionally sing a few of my favorite lines from "Jingle Bells" and "Deck the Halls." Eventually, I start to dance, shaking my hips and enjoying the hell out of the empty bakery.

When I spin around, that's when I remember I'm not alone. Burk is leaning against one of the bistro tables, a soft smile on his face as he watches me. My face turns as red as Rudolph's nose as he extends the hand holding the broom. "Broom mic?"

I burst out laughing and shake my head. "Wouldn't be the first time," I tell him, returning my attention to cleaning the counter, even though it was done as we closed down. "You know, if you're here, you'd be expected to join as a backup singer."

His face falls. "I couldn't just be a fan in the front row? Or maybe a groupie?"

My head is already shaking. "Nope, it's backup or nothing, Burkey Turkey."

"Well, maybe another time. I really should practice first, or maybe stretch or something?"

I double over in a fit of laughter. "Stretch? I'm not asking you to run the fifty-yard dash. I'll even get you the mop."

He just stands there and smiles, and my God, that smile. It could disarm Santa Claus of all his toys on Christmas Eve, that's for sure. Or maybe it just has some sort of magical powers to disarm me. Lord knows it does things to my body that I'm not accustomed to, especially by someone I consider a friend.

He shrugs his strong shoulders and returns his attention to his sweeping.

Twenty minutes later, all the cleaning is complete, and the bakery is officially ready to close up for the day. "Thank you for your help," I say, hanging the mop to dry on the hook.

"You're very welcome," he replies, walking over to the counter where he left his coat.

While he slips it on, I yawn as exhaustion hits me hard. Now that the bakery is clean, my body realizes it's been up since four this morning and is ready for bed. "Sorry," I mutter, trying to cover up my second yawn.

"You're tired. I'll let you get upstairs to bed," he replies, zipping his coat. I follow him as he makes his way to the front entrance, which is still unlocked from our arrival earlier. That's one of the beautiful things about Snowflake Falls. It's incredibly safe, and while I know I should have locked up behind us, I felt comfortable leaving it unlocked, but only because we were right here.

"Thanks for your help tonight."

"You're welcome," he says, stepping out onto the sidewalk, hands shoved in his pockets. Just before he turns to head to where he parked his vehicle, he asks, "Hey, Easy-Bake?"

"Yes?"

"Do you want to have dinner with me?"

My heart starts to pound a little harder in my chest. "Okay."

"Okay," he replies casually, but I can tell he seems to be relieved. "Can I call or text you?"

I nod, fighting not to smile.

"Do you have the same number?" he asks, his brown eyes shining a little brighter under the streetlights.

"I do."

He nods and flashes a grin. "I'll reach out."

Drawing my bottom lip between my teeth, I nod, feeling giddy like a schoolgirl when the boy you have a crush on talks to you. "All right."

"Have a good night, Easy-Bake."

"You too. Drive safe."

He heads down the sidewalk and rounds the corner, and my eyes follow him as far as they can before he disappears. On his ass, of course. It is one of his best assets.

Closing and securing the door, I turn the lights off and make my way to the back stairwell that leads to my apartment. With a ridiculous smile on my face, I wonder if I'll get any sleep tonight. Something tells me my thoughts and dreams will be consumed by a certain man with a disarming smile and an ass that makes me want to drop to my knees and beg for mercy.

I still don't exactly know what this dinner invitation means. Is it just two friends catching up, or does it hold a little more meaning?

My mind says one thing, but my heart is hoping for the other.

I suppose time will tell.

Chapter Six

Burk

"Take a quick lunch break," my cousin hollers at me after I load what feels like the thousandth tree so far today. "Gram made some chicken noodles and mashed potatoes up at the house. Take the UTV."

"I was gonna go in a bit and help a friend take her tree home," I tell him, earning me a look that tells me he's going to want more details.

"You can do both. Gram is waiting for you with some food, and then she's gonna run to visit Gramps. Run up and eat and then you can still take the tree when you need to."

I nod and wave, letting him know I heard him loud and clear. Pulling my work gloves off, I make my way to the UTV parked beside the big barn. Once I hop inside, I fire up the engine and take off toward the old farmhouse I'm currently staying in, my stomach growling from hunger.

Parking beside Gram's SUV, I turn off the machine and make my way into the garage. I take off my boots so I don't track snow inside the house before heading to the kitchen. "There you are," Gram says with a smile as I enter.

"I heard you made lunch," I say, leaning in and giving her a kiss on the cheek. "I only have a minute."

She spins around and grabs a bowl. "I sure did, and you need to take a few minutes to eat. I know today is one of the busiest days of the year, so I wanted to do something for you all before I left for the hospital."

"How was he this morning?" I ask, knowing Gram has already been in touch with the nurses on his floor.

"Ornery and itching to come home," she states with a chuckle.

I may not know my grandpa as of the last decade and a half, but I can see it. He was always the life of the party, the boisterous man with a work ethic that wouldn't quit. I'm sure it's killing him to be laid up in a hospital bed right now, especially this time of year. "I bet."

She fills my bowl to the brim and hands it off, scooping the rest of the pot into a plastic storage container to put in the fridge for later. I take a seat at the small island and shovel my food into my mouth. It's just after two in the afternoon, and the line of customers flocking to the farm shows no sign of slowing down.

"It looks pretty busy out there," Gram says, glancing out the kitchen window that overlooks the farm entrance.

"I don't remember it being like this when I was young," I confess.

She turns her attention my way and smiles. "It was, but you were usually running through the rows of trees, playing hide-and-seek, and helping yourself to cocoa and cookies from the snack shack."

I chuckle and nod. "Yeah, Klint and I had a lot of fun back then."

Gram is silent for a few seconds before she adds, "He really missed you when you left."

My throat grows dry as I gaze her way. "I missed him too."

Her smile is small and sad. "I'm glad you're here, Burk. We all are."

The dryness in my throat turns into a massive lump, which makes it a little difficult to breathe. "I'm glad to be here and help. I really missed this place...and you all."

"Well, you're here now, and that's what's important. What happened in the past stays there, right?"

I nod before taking another heaping forkful of mashed potato and chicken noodle goodness.

"Speaking of past, rumor has it you've reconnected with the Campbell girl."

My fork stalls halfway to my mouth. "Where'd you hear that?"

She just smiles back at me without saying a word.

"Right. Small town." I clear my throat. "I haven't talked to her in years. We're just catching up."

Gram nods and leans against the counter, watching me. "I understand that. You two were thick as thieves back in the day."

I continue to shovel my food into my mouth, not really knowing what else to say. Yes, Joy and I were good friends growing up. We played together all the time, especially at the tree farm. But we'd also ride bikes in town, play at the park, and watch movies together in her living room. We had a lot of fun, and I certainly missed that friendship after we moved away.

"You know, she hasn't dated much in the last few years. I'm sure it has a lot to do with opening her bakery and whatnot, but even before that, she didn't have many boyfriends. And when she did, it never seemed very serious."

My fork abandoned, my gaze returns to the woman standing before me. "Why are you telling me this?"

She shrugs. "Thought you'd want to know."

While a part of me does want to know if she's been dating anyone recently, it feels wrong to be discussing her like this in my gram's kitchen. I feel like any talk about her dating history should come from her, but I also can't help asking, "Anyone I know?"

Gram nods. "A few, I'm sure, since you went to school with most of them, but the one that sticks out was that Bransen boy. What's his name?"

The hairs on the back of my neck stand up, because only one name comes to mind, and it's not a good one. "Eli?"

"Yes, that's it!" Gram proclaims. "What a strange young man."

Well, that piques my interest, because in the years I knew Eli, I would never have thought he was strange. Cocky, yes. Opinionated, definitely. He was popular and bossed everyone around like they were his little school-aged minions. I never got along with him, mostly because everything I said was always wrong in his eyes.

Before I can ask more questions, my walkie-talkie squawks to life. "Burk, you're being summoned to the tree farm. There's a beautiful young woman here, ready to pick out her tree," Ray says, making me smile. Instantly I know he's talking about his youngest daughter.

"On my way," I reply, shoveling the rest of my lunch into my mouth and quickly chewing.

"How you can eat like that is beyond me," Gram mutters, shaking her head.

"I had to eat fast when we were younger or Klint would have taken my food," I retort. Klint had a huge appetite when we were kids, always eating twice as much as the rest of us. How he doesn't weigh twice as much as he does is still unknown.

Gram laughs hard. "That boy could sure eat, right? He ate everything that wasn't nailed down," she teases, taking my bowl off the table.

"I can rinse it," I state. "You don't have to pick up after me."

She just grins that grandmotherly little smile I remember from my childhood. "Hush, boy. I haven't seen you in a few years, so if I want to take care of you, I will."

It was more than a few years, but who's counting...

"Thank you for lunch," I tell her, meeting her at the sink and pressing a kiss to her cheek.

"You're very welcome. Now, go so you can help that pretty young woman with her tree selection," Gram says, and by the gleam in her eyes, she knows exactly who I'm off to assist. "Tell Joy I said hello."

"I will," I reply, moving to the door so I can put on my winter clothes and boots. "Tell Gramps I said hello too."

"As soon as he moves to the rehab facility, he would love a visit."

Again, my throat gets a little tight from emotion. "I'd like that."

"Good," she replies, reaching for a hand towel and swinging it at me. "Now, go. Help Joy with her tree." She throws in a wink for good measure before returning her attention to the dishes in the sink.

I quickly go to the garage and redress before heading out to the UTV. I'd be lying if I said there wasn't a little extra spring in my step—or a little extra speed in my drive—as I make my way to the barn. Parking the utility vehicle, I smile the moment I see Joy over by her dad and walk that way.

"Hey," I say as I approach.

"Hi. Sorry to interrupt your lunch," Joy replies.

"You're fine. Gram just made me eat before she went to the hospital to visit Gramps."

"I'll leave you two to it," Ray announces, leaning in and kissing his daughter on the cheek before patting me on the back. He takes off toward the pay hut to help the next customer, leaving us alone.

"I expected your dad to help you pick your tree," I tell her as we make our way to retrieve one of the sleds.

"Umm, he told me it would be easier if you did it."

I stop walking and just look at her. "What?"

Joy shrugs and chuckles. "Honestly, I think this was his way of, well, like, putting us...together."

A huge smile stretches my lips. I knew I liked that man. "Well, I'm happy to help cut it down and then deliver it to your house."

"If you don't have time, we can just throw it in the bed of Dad's truck and I can take it to my apartment, like I had planned."

Reaching the rope of one of the remaining sleds, I say, "No, you're fine. I only took about ten minutes of lunch time, so it's no big deal to help you get it into your place."

"If you're sure," she says, falling in line beside me as we head toward the sections of trees available to cut down. "You're pretty busy today."

I nod. "They were lined up when I got up here to open the gate."

"Dad always says this weekend and the one right before Christmas are the busiest, and that's always weird to me. I mean, why wait until right before the holiday to decorate a tree? You're missing out on so many nights of prime tree light enjoyment."

I have to grin, because of course she would feel that way. I'm surprised she doesn't have her tree up before now, if I'm being honest. But I suppose she already has one in her bakery to enjoy all day long. "I'll take your word for it," I state, thinking back to my small house back in South Carolina and the lack of a Christmas tree over the last few years.

She stops walking, halting my own progress. "Burkey Turkey, I need to ask you a very important question, and I need you to be one-hundred-percent honest with me."

The corner of my mouth ticks. "Of course."

"Do you put up a tree? Back home?"

I swallow hard and meet her gaze. "I'm usually too busy to worry about it."

She gasps so loud, I swear you could hear it in the next county. "What?" She starts marching away toward a section of Fraser fir trees.

"I'm sorry, Easy-Bake, but December is one of my busiest times. I usually work fourteen to sixteen hour days, and sometimes more right before the holiday."

She's already shaking her head, looking so fucking cute in her stocking cap and annoyed, shocked face. "No excuse, Burkey Turkey. I can't believe you don't put up a tree."

I sigh as she turns into one of the rows and starts scanning the trees. "If I'm being honest, it's never felt very Christmassy there. I mean, it's South Carolina. It rarely snows, and if it does it's gone before you can truly enjoy it. The landscape is just different there." I don't tell her how much I hated the first few Christmases there. I missed Snowflake Falls, at least during the holidays.

"But on the other side, we have beach season."

Joy sticks out her tongue. "Beach season. Gross."

I bark out a laugh. "It's not that bad," I assure her.

"It sounds terrible," she retorts, stopping in front of a tree. "This is the one."

I look at what she's pointing at and nod in agreement. "It's pretty ugly."

She giggles the sweetest sound. "It is. That's why it's perfect."

"All right," I reply, dropping the rope and reaching for the handsaw in the bucket attached to the sled.

She doesn't say anything as I lie down on the snow-covered ground and get into position. With saw in hand, I start to cut.

"When Eve and I were little, we'd spend what felt like hours finding the perfect tree. We wanted the perfect fullness, the perfect height, the perfect coloring. We wanted everything...well, perfect. Then we both got older and decided that these less than perfect trees deserve love too. I've definitely had my fair share of Charlie Brown trees over the years."

"Coming down," I holler as I cut through the trunk and give the tree a shove away from where I'm lying. Hopping up off the ground, I make sure the saw is put away and smile when I realize Joy has already spread out the netting to wrap the tree.

Once the saw is secured in the bucket, I pick the tree up off the ground and place it in the middle of the net. I quickly get her selection wrapped up and on the sled, ready to transport back to the pay hut.

"So, I was thinking," Joy starts, as we make our way back.

"About?" I ask when she doesn't continue.

"What are you doing after you get off work?"

"Nothing," I tell her, thinking about later tonight. I know Gram will be back at some point, but I was hoping to relax and have a beer. Even though I knew I was in for some manual labor, I never expected to work so damn hard this weekend. The level of respect I have for my grandparents—especially my grandpa, who is still working the front line of the farm—tripled now that I'm here and doing the job.

"Well, I was wondering if you wanted to come over. For dinner." And then she seems to quickly add, "As a thank you for helping me with the tree."

Suddenly, all thoughts of relaxing with a beer tonight fly right out the window.

We continue walking, and I nod to an excited family of four on their way to find a tree. "We don't close tonight until six," I tell her when the others have passed.

"I know it's late, so if you don't want to, I understand."

I open my mouth to reply, but we're suddenly surrounded by people. A little boy comes running up to Joy, throwing his arms around her legs and squeezing. "Hi, Miss Joy!"

"Hello, Alton, how are you?"

"Dood! I come get a tree!"

"Me too," she tells him, pointing to the wrapped tree on our sled.

"Bye!" he hollers, taking off running to an older woman and man who look really familiar.

Joy clears her throat and walks to the pay hut. I let her do her thing, stealing a glance at the older man, woman, child, and a younger man who scoops up the boy and spins him around.

When Joy finishes paying, we start to make our way over to where my grandpa's old farm truck is parked. I make sure to radio to the crew that I'm making a delivery so they know I'm off-site for a short time.

"We can use my dad's," Joy states.

"Yeah, but then I couldn't drive this old beauty, and I've wanted to drive it since I was a kid," I tell her. I leave out the part I drove it around the farm a few times when I was younger, but never legally on the roadway.

Joy climbs in the passenger door and buckles up. Once I make sure the tree isn't going anywhere, I do the same and fire up the engine. I take the side entrance out of the farm and head toward downtown Snowflake Falls. "That man and woman looked familiar," I say, asking without coming out and asking who they are.

"Do you remember Amy Samson?"

As soon as she says the name it hits me. "Of course. They are her parents."

Joy nods, looking out the side window. "Amy and I became good friends after high school. She married a guy from out of town. That was Nick with them."

"And that little boy must be her son," I assume.

"Yes, that's Alton." There's a brief pause before she adds, "Amy passed away two weeks after she gave birth. She had a brain aneurism."

"What? Shit," I mutter, feeling terrible for asking.

"Sally brings Alton to the bakery every Thursday after preschool for a chocolate milk and sweet treat."

I remain silent, because I don't know what to say. Hearing about the loss of a classmate hits me hard in the chest. I may not have finished school with Amy, but we were classmates during my time here. She was a sweet girl, and I can see why she and Joy became close after graduation.

"You can park around back in the alley," she tells me, and before I know it, I'm pulling up to the door marked with the bakery logo and a sign for deliveries.

I turn off the truck and hop out, slipping my gloves back on to grab the tree. "Ready, Easy-Bake?"

She rewards me with a big grin that makes her eyes twinkle. "The question is, are you ready, Burkey Turkey?"

Her question feels flirty. Very flirty.

Oh, I'm definitely ready.

But I can't help but wonder, am I really?

Am I ready for Joy Campbell?

Chapter Seven

Joy

I don't know why I suddenly feel playful, but I do. First with the dinner invitation, which he hasn't accepted or declined yet, and then with the flirty question about being ready.

Climbing out of the cab of the truck, I meet him at the tailgate, but instantly realize I need to get the doors unlocked first. By the time I have the back entrance of the building opened, he's there, tree thrown over his shoulder like some sort of holiday lumberjack. "I was going to help you carry it," I tell him, holding open the door so he can enter.

"I got it," he insists, offering a wink as he walks inside the building.

Closing the door behind me, Burk starts to take the tree up to my apartment. It isn't until he's at the landing in front of the next door that I realize the issue. He's in front of me, and I need to get past him to get that door unlocked too.

"I guess we didn't think this one through," I state, just as he's realizing the issue.

"Oops," he comments with a gravelly chuckle that makes my nipples hard and a wave of warmth rush between my legs. "Umm, can you slip past behind me?" He turns to the side, sandwiching the tree between his chest and the wall.

"I think so." I shift to my side and carefully try to slip behind him on the stairs. Of course, my entire front brushes his back, and even though we're wearing coats and cold-weather gear, I swear I feel the heat of his body.

Or maybe it's just my sudden overanxious body that seems to home in on his physique and nearness.

"Sorry," I mutter as my boobs brush against him. Of course, I'm sure he can't really feel them, considering the layers of clothes, but still. I feel like an apology is necessary since the last time I saw him he had braces and skinned-up knees from wiping out on his skateboard, and I was what was referred to as a carpenter's dream back in my teenage years.

Flat as a board and never been nailed.

I didn't grow boobs until I was about twenty.

Of course, I wasn't actually called that until later in high school, but whatever. I was still a skinny, awkward girl with no curves, who liked to play outside with her male best friend instead of going shopping or doing hair and nails.

"You're fine," he declares. Out of the corner of my eye, I swear I see a smirk on his lips.

Heat stains my cheeks and there's a touch of a shake to my fingers as I place the key in the lock and turn it. The familiarity of home washes over me as I step inside and plaster myself against the wall to ensure he has enough room to enter. Fortunately, the doorway opens into the kitchen, which has plenty of space for the both of us to not be all up against each other.

Or unfortunately the more I think about it.

"Umm, I have the stand set up over there," I say, ripping off my stocking cap and pointing to the narrow floor-to-ceiling windows in the living room.

Burk moves in the direction I indicated and carefully places the tree in the stand. He drops to his knees before I can offer to assist and tightens the screw system holding the tree in place. Then, he removes a knife from his pocket and gets to work at cutting the netting off. When the tree falls back out, I can't help but smile when I see there aren't many damaged branches, and it looks pretty good.

"Thank you," I tell him, super excited and ready to start decorating.

"Well, it's not a perfect tree, but I think you did a good job," he tells me, standing back and admiring the naked pine.

"I really appreciate you helping me get it home." I don't know why I'm suddenly nervous. Perhaps it's for the simple fact he's standing in my living room, in my private space, and all I can smell is fresh pine and a hint of his masculine soap.

He reaches down and gathers up the cut netting and rolls it into a ball. "So, about earlier. You had asked me to dinner, before we were interrupted by Amy's son."

That nervousness inside me seems to duplicate, growing like a weed. I've never been super outgoing, but I've never considered myself shy either. I mean, I was in theater and art, for crying out loud. And right now, I feel anything but confident. Maybe I shouldn't have asked him to dinner.

"If the offer still stands, I'd love to have dinner with you. Though, I did offer to take you out somewhere so we can catch up."

"I love to cook," I blurt out. Feeling heat mark my cheeks, I add, "Well, baking is more my forte, but I do enjoy making a few signature dishes. Plus, I really want to decorate my tree."

He chuckles. "Okay, what can I bring?"

"Just yourself."

He nods. "All right. I get off at six, and I'll run up to the house and take a quick shower. I can be here around six thirty."

You know the scene in *Home Alone*, where Kevin outsmarts the criminals by throwing a party? My heart feels like that right now. It's as if I'm rockin' around the Christmas tree.

"No rush. It'll be ready when you get here." I pray I don't sound as breathless as I feel.

The smile he gives me makes my entire body come alive with need, and even though I should be embarrassed for reacting this way because he's my friend, I can't help it. He's just so...adorable.

"I better get back to the farm before they send the cavalry," he jokes, but I know there's a little truth to his statement. They may not come looking for him, but they'll definitely wonder what's taking so long.

As he moves to the door, I reach out my hand. "I can take that and throw it away."

He places the balled up netting in my palms, and I swear the moment his fingers brush against my skin, some sort of explosion happens. Like sizzling sparklers on the Fourth of July.

"See you in a little while?" he asks when he makes it to my door.

"Yep."

He flashes me another panty-melting grin before exiting my apartment, leaving me in a puddle of eggnog and faulty Christmas lights. I'm going to get shocked. Bad.

He's just a friend...

I keep repeating that over and over as I prepare for Burk's arrival. He should be here any minute, and I'm excited. That's the only way to describe it. I'm anxious to continue getting to know the man he's become. What little time we've spent together over the last couple of days has been enjoyable, and it seems easy to fall into the same state of friendship we used to have back when he lived here.

The only problem is, what I'm feeling for him isn't quite so friendly, if you know what I mean.

I'm completely attracted to him.

I give the slow cooker contents a quick stir and replace the lid. Garlic bread is in the oven, and the table is set. I prepared one of my favorite chicken pasta dishes tonight, one I don't make as much as I'd like, mostly because it makes enough to feed an army, and while I don't mind leftovers, I don't want to eat it for a week straight either.

A distant knock sounds on the back door, so I quickly move to my apartment door. Just as I'm pulling it open to wave him up, Burk is stepping through the lower doorway and glances up. "Hey."

"Hi," I reply. "Usually, I keep that door locked."

He nods in understanding and engages the locks, both the knob one and the deadbolt, before returning his attention my way and climbing the stairs. It's the first time I notice one of his hands is holding a plant, and I can't help but smile.

As he reaches the platform in front of me, he grins and extends his hand. "This is for you."

The small potted poinsettia plant with its beautiful white leaves is a stark contrast against the dark coat he's wearing. The red and white ceramic vase resembling Santa's coat will look perfect in my holiday decorated apartment. "Thank you," I reply as I take the pot. "Come on in. Dinner's ready."

My apartment seems so much smaller with Burk inside. He's tall, sure, but everything around me just feels tighter with him here. It's not unwelcome, not in the least. In fact, his presence is the exact opposite. I *want* him here. With me.

I place the potted poinsettia on the counter and check the garlic bread in the oven. "You haven't decorated your tree."

I turn around, knowing this was going to be one of the first things he'd notice. "No, I, uh, hoped you'd be willing to help me."

"Really?" His brown eyes are wide with anticipation.

I shrug and reach for a hand towel, wringing it in my hands. "Yeah, well, it would be nice to have some help with it. You're tall, you know. You can wrap the top of the tree with the lights," I state with a chuckle.

He grins. "I'd be honored to assist."

"Great," I beam back just as the timer goes off.

Pulling the warm bread from the oven, I quickly place our meal in the center of the table. "What can I get you to drink?"

"Just water, please," he states, moving toward the table. He doesn't sit, however, just waits for me to join him.

I can tell he's waiting for me to take a seat first, so I place two glasses of water on the table and pull out my chair. Only when I do that does he take the available seat across from me. My table is a small two-seater, but it fits the space and my lifestyle perfectly.

The gentleman that he is, Burk offers me the spoon and waits for me to place a scoop of the Italian chicken pasta bake onto my plate before taking some for himself. "This smells amazing," he tells me, placing two hearty spoonfuls on his plate.

"Thank you. It's a pretty simple recipe, but it just makes so much. If you like it, I may be sending some home with you for leftovers," I reply with a chuckle, grabbing a piece of garlic bread and holding the plate out for him.

"I wouldn't say no to that," he replies, grabbing two pieces of bread. "Gram has been cooking for all of us, but she usually spends dinners at the hospital with Gramps, leaving me to fend for myself."

"How's he doing?" I ask, even though I got an update from my dad earlier today.

We spend our meal talking about the positive steps his grandpa is taking toward recovery, as well as Burk getting to know his grandma and extended family again. I'm sure it's weird being back here when you lost so many years and have hardly spoken to any of them. I couldn't imagine not having my parents right there—literally and figuratively. And Eve? The thought of not being close to my sister makes my stomach drop.

By the time our bellies are full, it feels so comfortable and familiar to be sitting with him at the table that I wish I could start the meal over and do it all again. This is exactly when I realize asking him to help me decorate my Christmas tree was the right move. It's an incredibly personal and slightly intimate gesture, sure, but more than that it feels like I'm sharing a piece of myself with my best friend.

"So, what do you say? You ready to help me decorate that tree?" I ask the moment the leftovers are placed into two plastic containers and slipped into the refrigerator.

He props his hip against the counter, his eyes smiling with mirth. "Are you going to boss me around and tell me I'm doing it wrong?"

"Absolutely," I confirm.

Burk barks out a laugh and claps his hands together. "Well, I do love it when a gorgeous woman gets a little bossy."

My heart flutters in my chest, and I feel my cheeks blush. My brain crosses the invisible line in the sand that separates appropriate from inappropriate, and it doesn't seem to bother me one bit that I'm standing on what is probably considered the wrong side. All I can think about is being intimate with him and throwing out a few bossy demands.

I don't hate the idea.

Not to mention the fact he called me gorgeous. It's not the first time he's flattered me with a compliment, and I'm praying it's not the last. Will that add to my confusion? To the blurred line between friendship and more than friendship? Absolutely. Do I seem to care or want it to stop?

Nope.

"Come on, Burkey Turkey. I have totes upon totes of the good stuff," I tell him, walking past where he stands and moving into the living room side of the open floor plan.

That's when I feel his eyes on my ass.

Unable to resist, I glance over my shoulder and confirm my suspicions. Burk's eyes are glued to my backside as we make our way to where my naked tree awaits. So what do I do? Add a little extra swing to my hips, and when he glances up, his brown eyes are a bit darker and filled with something that resembles lust. I go ahead and wink, letting him know I not only caught him, but I'm A-OK with it.

"Holy crap, all this goes on your tree?" he asks, turning his attention to the four large totes stacked on the floor.

"Sure does."

He runs his hand down his face as he gapes at the mountain of holiday décor. "How? I mean, that's enough for five or six trees, Easy-Bake."

Grinning widely, I respond, "Well, Burkey Turkey, watch and be amazed."

I pull my phone from my pocket and turn up the volume on my speaker. The room fills with the classic holiday hits I love so much, and even though I'm already in a spectacular mood, it just seems to lighten even more, and the beat washes over me and moves my hips. Just like it does downstairs when I'm prepping and baking, because when the music washes over me, it makes me happy.

And happy people dance.

I open the top tote and smile at the strings of twinkling white lights inside. Burk moves behind me, his body hovering very close to my back and I can feel his heat. His head appears over my shoulder as he gazes down into the tote. "That's a lot of lights," he murmurs, almost to himself.

"Twelve hundred," I announce proudly.

He whistles his shock. "How do you not start a fire?"

I chuckle and start pulling the light wheels out of the tote. "Well, I don't leave the tree on when I'm gone, and I make sure it's well watered so it doesn't get too dry. Plus, they're LED."

He exhales slowly, his warm breath fanning across my neck. As he steps back, he claps his hands and rubs his palms together. "Well, I love a good challenge. Let's do this."

We start at the top and he follows my lead as I begin sliding the lights between the branches. We work side by side for several minutes, inserting the first two strands of white lights and listening to Christmas music.

"Can I ask you a question?"

I glance over to where he's concentrating on making sure every strand of lighting is in the perfect placement. "Of course."

"How come there's no Mr. Easy-Bake?"

I shrug, feeling the shift of his gaze from the tree to me. "Haven't really found 'the one,' you know?"

He nods in understanding. "Me neither."

My throat is thick, but I can't help but ask, "Have you ever come close?"

Burk pauses before finishing placing the rest of the strand in his hand. "Once."

My interest is piqued now. "Really?"

He shrugs and rocks back on his heels. "Yeah. Someone I met in my early-twenties."

"What happened?" I find myself asking, even though I'm not sure I want the answer.

"We just weren't as good of a match as I thought we were. She didn't want kids, and I did."

He doesn't elaborate, and I know I'm not going to get any more information. Not that I'm owed it, because I'm not. It's his past, his life, and he doesn't have to share it all with me. I'm just a friend, someone from a former life before he moved to South Carolina, and I'm not privileged to every single detail of his life, dating or otherwise.

After a few seconds, he adds, "She didn't like what I did for a living."

Okay, I wasn't expecting that...

"What? Why?" I'm completely confused about why someone wouldn't find value in what he does.

"Her father was a banker, and she thought I would make more money going into her family business."

Confusion washes over me. "That's...dumb. Has she not seen your work? I got online last night and found your social pages and website and saw even more photos. Your work is beautiful; that's the only way to describe it."

He cracks a cheeky grin. "You social media stalked me?"

I open my mouth, but all I do is stick my foot in it. "Uhhh..."

"It's okay, Easy-Bake. I social media stalked you too."

"You did?"

He shrugs. "That first night after I dropped by the bakery. Gram was still at the hospital, so I did a quick search of your bakery."

"Oh." Knowing he searched me out and saw my social media pages makes me a little giddy, and if he weren't staring at me right now, I'd probably do a little happy dance.

"Didn't see any guy pics on your socials," he states, not as a question.

I slip the rest of the final strand of white lights onto the tree and step back. "No, no guy pics anywhere."

He moves to stand directly beside me. "Good."

Curiosity gets the better of me, and I turn to face him. "Good?"

He shrugs. "That just means there's no one in your life right now I need to worry about."

My heart is beating so hard, I'm sure the Grinch could hear it all the way up at Mount Crumpit. "Worry about?" I whisper, trying to get my bearings.

He just grins before reaching out and swiping a lock of hair from my forehead. His fingers leave a trail of heat in their wake as they brush across my skin. "It might make me an asshole, but I'm a little relieved you're not dating anyone."

"Why?" The voice asking the question doesn't even sound like my own.

"Because that means I don't have to share you with anyone else while I'm here. I get you. All of you."

Well, okay then.

He seems to find humor in my lack of words and smiles so brightly you don't even need the lights on my tree to brighten the room. His smile alone does the job just fine.

"Come on, Easy-Bake. Let's decorate."

Chapter Eight

Burk

It's taking every ounce of self-control I have not to kiss her. From the moment I handed off the poinsettia and she smiled in appreciation; I've been fighting a mental battle to remain gentlemanly and respectful. I want to kiss her, and I want it more than I want my next breath of air.

"Oh my God," I blurt out, pulling a familiar ornament out of the last tote of holiday decorations.

Joy's face blushes dark as she bites her bottom lip and looks away.

"You still have it." It's not a question. It can't be. The proof is in my hand.

I stare down at the handmade ornament, and I'm transported right back to the day I gave it to her. She hadn't been feeling well and missed two days of school. On the third day, a Saturday, I was working with my dad and uncle at the tree farm and went to the craft station to see if they needed anything. They were helping kids make popsicle stick ornaments, and I decided I needed to make one for Joy.

I chose the reindeer design, which was really just an upside-down triangle with some pipe cleaner antlers, two googly eyes, and a red pom-pom for the nose. I took extra time making sure it was proportionally correct and even adding some silver glitter glue sparkles around the nose because I knew Joy would love it.

And when I handed it to her that Monday she returned to school? She hugged that reindeer to her chest and said it was the best reindeer ornament she'd ever seen and would keep it forever.

I had forgotten all about this damn reindeer...until now.

"Well, yeah."

I look up from the gift I had made her when I was eight or nine years old and stumble to find the right words. "You did say you'd keep it forever."

She flashes a sweet smile. "I did, and I will. It was the best gift to get after having the stomach flu for three or four days."

I hand it over to her and watch as she takes the first ornament to the tree and hangs it right in the middle at shoulder level. "I feel like I can slay dragons now. That's prime placement, Easy-Bake."

"It is, but now I need to move it because your head is swelling and there's no room for that here, Burkey Turkey."

I bark out a laugh and make my move as she reaches for the ornament, playfully ready to move it to a new position. Wrapping my hands around her wrists gently, I pull her back, making sure my reindeer stays right where it is. Joy wiggles and twists her arms to try to dislodge my hold. All that seems to do is brush her perfect ass against my groin.

Instinctively, I wrap my arms around her frame and pull her back against my chest. Her back presses to my chest, and a wave of desire rushes through my veins. I can feel my cock getting hard, and even though I should put some distance between us, I can't seem to make myself move.

Joy holds completely still, her body pressed firmly against mine. She breathes in deeply and slowly lets it out. If she can feel my growing erection, she doesn't let on, but honestly, there's no way she can miss it. It's not likely I smuggled a baseball bat into the apartment, and if I did, she definitely would have seen it.

Holding her against my chest feels...right.

Should it?

I'm not sure, but I don't hate it. Joy has always been my friend, but now, all I want to do is kiss her lips and get very *un*-friendly, if you know what I mean. Or would that be too friendly? Hell if I know, but I crave more from this woman than I've ever needed before.

Just as I'm trying to figure out how to casually get us out of this position we're in, she starts to turn. I go to drop my arms but pause when I feel hers wrap around my lower back. Now we're standing chest to chest, and I can see the rapid rise and fall of hers as she greedily sucks in shallow breaths.

A shiver sweeps through her. "Are you cold?"

Slowly, she shakes her head, keeping those mesmerizing eyes locked on mine.

My throat is thick, and it's suddenly hard to breathe with her in my arms like this. It's comfortable and familiar in a way I've never experienced, and frankly, I don't want to stop.

I clear my throat and decide to man up and ask the burning question. "Is it weird I want to kiss you?"

"No," she replies softly, her eyelashes seeming to flutter as she closes her eyes for a brief moment. "If I'm being honest, I've been hoping you'd kiss me since you walked in the door."

My chest seems to swell with excitement as my eyes zero in on her mouth. Her tongue slips out and slides along her plump lips, ensuring all blood in my body starts to move south of the beltline.

I ignore the way my pants feel a little too tight in the crotch area and just submerge myself in this moment. It probably sounds juvenile or silly, but everything around me fades away. The holiday music, the twinkling lights of Joy's tree, everything. The only thing left is us. Together.

The moment my lips brush against hers, gentle and slightly hesitant, I realize instantly this isn't just any kiss. The mere touch of our lips together is like a lightning strike, a hard punch to the solar plexus. It steals my breath, my sanity, and every bit of composure I have to keep this in check. First kisses should be PG, but what I'm feeling is on the complete opposite on the rating scale.

Joy mewls against my lips and opens her mouth. The moment she does, my tongue slides in, tasting her for the first time. She tastes sweet, like sugar and spice, and I'm certain I'll never get enough of her.

Her hands grip the back of my hoodie, as if anchoring herself to me. As I gently deepen the kiss, my hands travel to her neck, my fingers sliding up into her hair. It's just as silky and soft as I imagined, and suddenly, all I can envision is seeing that hair splayed across a white pillowcase.

Pushing those images from my brain, I slow the kiss and pull back, watching the pure bliss as she smiles. Her eyes are still closed, and it's as if she's replaying every moment of our first kiss in her head.

Yes, first kiss, because now that I've had a taste, there's no way I won't want to kiss her every chance I get.

Joy clears her throat and opens her eyes. They're still glossy as she murmurs, "I wasn't expecting that."

I don't have to ask her to elaborate. "I wasn't either."

Her cheeks darken as she gives me a shy grin. "I liked it."

"Me too," I confess, already replaying it in my own mind.

With Herculean strength, I release my hold on her and take a step back. If I were to look down, I'm sure she'd be able to tell just how much that kiss affected me, so I quickly start running math stats through my head, trying to curb my erection.

"So, what do you say we finish this masterpiece?" I ask, glancing over at her tree.

A wide smile spreads across her face. "Let's do it."

Those three words don't exactly help the problem I'm having in my pants, but I somehow manage to not maul her and show her exactly what I'm dreaming about if we were to *do it*.

She hands over a few more handmade ornaments, and we get to work.

"Did Mr. James get back into his classroom?" I ask, sitting back and smiling from ear to ear as she recounts a story from her English class freshman year.

"He did, but only because he had to do the walk of shame to the front office and tell them he somehow locked himself out of his classroom."

I shake my head, putting as many faces with the names she gives me as she shares stories from her time in high school after I left for the East Coast. "Who actually locked him out?"

Joy shifts in her seat. "Eli."

Of course he did. Eli was popular and everyone loved him, but I found him to be the biggest jerk in our class. "Should have guessed."

She gives me a knowing grin, and I already know what I'm going to ask her. "So...I might have heard something. About you and Eli."

She gives me a slow nod. I can tell by the look on her face, he's not her favorite topic of conversation, but she doesn't shy away from the subject. "Yeah, that was...a mistake? No, I can't really say that because I learned a lot through that relationship."

"How so?" I ask.

"Well, I realized I wanted to be with someone who values my time and company. Who enjoys a night in, sitting and watching our favorite shows just as much as going out and hanging with friends. Oh, and someone who doesn't cheat on me."

A wave of anger washes over me as her words sink in. "What a fucking douche."

She snorts a laugh and nods in agreement. "That he is." After a moment, she continues, "We were in very different places in our lives. Eli was always the life of the party and wanted to go out. All the time. I was starting my bakery, so my hours didn't fit his schedule well."

That's horseshit. He should have gone out of his way to support her and her new business venture, and that included finding the time to be with her during her restricted hours.

"Well, I actually prefer nights in over nights out," I find myself saying, earning me another one of her breathtaking smiles.

"Yeah?"

"Yep. And I'd never cheat. Only a real asshole does that. He's definitely on Santa's naughty list for the rest of his life."

She giggles and nods before sobering. "Totally. Funny, though, both my sister and I found cheaters."

"Really?"

"Yeah, she was engaged to Andrew Detweiler before she reconnected with John. He cheated on her with the funeral home's office assistance, who was like eight years older than him, *married*, and had three kids."

My mouth drops open. "Jesus."

"Yep," Joy confirms, taking a sip of her eggnog. "Eli and I had only been dating about a year. He apparently was very *friendly* with one of the bartenders at the place he liked to hang out, if you know what I mean."

"Unfortunately, I know exactly what you mean," I mutter, wishing the jerk was standing in front of me so I could punch him in the face for being such a douche. "You're better off."

She nods. "I agree completely. I don't regret it, because I learned so much about myself as I dealt with his betrayal, and it's all behind me now."

"I'm glad," I tell her, happy to hear she's in a good place in life. "So where is the cheater at these days?" I find myself asking curiously.

"Oh, he's around. He's the PE teacher at the high school."

I snort in disgust. "Of course he is." Eli was very athletic and loved to remind those who weren't how superior he was with his natural ability.

"I rarely see him though. He doesn't come into the bakery at all, and I don't exactly frequent the bars."

I can't help but wonder if I'll run into the asshole at some point during my time here. It's inevitable, I'm sure, but I just hope I'm able to contain my comments about what a tool he is. As much as I'd love to tell him off—or better yet, blacken his eye—it's not the impression I want to leave with Joy or my family.

Joy yawns, and I realize it's time for me to go. I finish off my eggnog and rise to take my glass to the kitchen. "Just leave it in the sink. I'll take care of it tomorrow," she informs me.

I grin because, even though I'm still getting to know the woman she became, I always had a pretty good read on her through her youth, and there is no way she'll leave those dishes until tomorrow. I'd bet my favorite hand plane on it.

"So, I was thinking," I start, giving her my full attention. "I haven't been to the festival in years. Well, besides watching the princess competition with you all. But I'd love to go. You know, the whole food, rides, and maybe some ice skating?"

Her eyes light up just how I hoped they would. Joy's favorite part of the festival when we were younger was ice skating, and we'd spend every chance we got circling that frozen rink. "Yeah?"

"Would you like to go with me? I know we both have work schedules to contend with, but I'm usually off at a decent time on Saturdays. I could probably even ask my uncle if I can leave a little earlier, if we're not busy."

She watches me with assessing eyes before asking, "So, is this like...a date?"

"Yes," I blurt out almost immediately.

"Okay." Joy clears her throat and adds, "I'm usually done by four on Saturdays, so I can be ready anytime after that."

I nod, trying to hide my excitement. "How about we keep the time open for now, but at the very latest six thirty or seven. That's if I can't get off work early and help closedown at six."

"That sounds great." She's beaming an award-winning smile, and I can't help but feel this rush of eagerness and happiness, knowing it's because of me, of my invitation.

"Is it okay if I text you? Throughout the week?"

She nods, nibbling on her bottom lip as she fights a grin. "Absolutely."

"Okay. Good." I walk toward the door, slipping on my coat as I go and hesitate when I reach it. I don't want to leave, but I know it's time. The last thing I'd want to do is overstay my welcome, especially when we're getting to know each other again.

Joy moves to stand beside me, gazing up at me with big eyes, filled with longing. This rush of exhilaration is new, and not just because it's her. I've never felt this raw before. It's fresh and exciting, and even though there's a touch of scary mixed in, the anticipation overcomes it. I just want...more. More time, more kisses, more...Joy.

"Would it be all right if I kissed you again?" I find myself asking, my eyes locked on her lips.

"I was hoping you would," she murmurs, stepping closer and wrapping her arms around my waist.

Our bodies press into each other, her curves melting against me, as I claim her lips with my own. This kiss is...perfect. It's gentle, yet firm, urgent, yet leisurely. I know those are contradictory, but that's how it feels. Every time our mouths meet, it's heaven.

And so fucking right.

I don't kiss her nearly as long as I want, mostly because I'd be here all night. Instead, I press a featherlight kiss on the corner of her mouth and pull away. "Good night, Joy," I whisper.

"Night, Burk."

I step back and grab the knob, twisting open the door and stepping through the entryway. As I make my way down the steps, I feel the weight of her gaze on me. "I'll lock this door when I go," I tell her, even though I know she'll need to come down and secure the secondary deadbolt lock.

"Thank you," she replies.

Finally, I turn around and look up. She's standing there, leaning against the doorjamb. "Thanks again for dinner," I say, holding up the leftovers.

She grins. "You're welcome. Thanks for helping me decorate my tree."

"My pleasure," I assure. "Have a good day tomorrow."

"You too."

I nod, realizing I'm doing all I can to draw out every second of time I can. Lifting my free hand, I offer a wave, before opening the door, relocking the knob so it's secured once I pull it closed, and step out into the cold Colorado night.

Walking to my rental, I climb inside and start the ignition. Fresh snow starts to fall, and even though I'm not used to it as part of my normal winter anymore, it feels so damn good to see those little flakes falling from the sky.

Damn, I've missed this.

Missed the snow and missed Snowflake Falls.

Missed my family and the farm.

And yes, I've missed the hell out of Joy Campbell.

Even now, driving away from her apartment, I miss her.

That should scare the hell out of me, but it doesn't. I'm not exactly sure why, but it feels more like a homecoming than anything else. Like I've been missing a piece of something important in my life for a very long time.

And now that I'm here?

Those pieces are clicking into place.

One very big problem remains.
My time here has an expiration date.

Chapter Nine

Joy

I flop over and try to adjust myself against my pillow, searching for sleep to claim me. Unfortunately, as it's been for the last thirty minutes, I can't seem to calm my racing mind. I even try to recite measurement conversions to ease my thoughts, but it's not working. In everything Burk worms his way into it.

Reaching for my phone, I hesitate just before the device is in my hand. I shouldn't be texting him. I'm sure he's home relaxing, and the last thing he needs is me interrupting his night with chitchat.

But then I recall how he seemed to be at war with himself as he was leaving, like he didn't want to go. In fact, he'd probably still be sitting in my living room, chatting, if he hadn't noticed my yawns. I'm certain he caught on to the fact it was nearing my bedtime. My body starts to shut down at the same time every night, thanks to years of getting up at four in the morning.

I reach for the phone again, this time grabbing on to it and tapping the screen. Maybe sending him a quick message will appease my overactive brain, and I'll be able to fall asleep finally.

> **Me:** Hey, just checking to make sure you made it home ok.

The dancing dots appear almost instantly.

> **Burk:** I did. Snow is starting to come down fast now. It's been so long since I've gotten to see this kind of snow, it's refreshing and beautiful.

> **Me:** It doesn't snow in SC?

> **Burk:** It does, but not like this. And we're more toward the east side of the state, toward the ocean, so we don't get it as often.

Me: I can't imagine living somewhere with no snow.

Burk: It definitely took some getting used to, but the beaches and ocean waves make up for it.

Me: I guess, but that still doesn't sound as appealing.

Burk: How come you're not sleeping?

Me: Wanted to make sure you arrived back at your grandparents' safely?

Burk: Is that a question? *insert laughing emoji*

Me: Fine. I was thinking about you.

Burk: I've been thinking about you nonstop too.

Me: What does this mean?

Burk: It means we have a lot of history and are enjoying getting to know each other again. At least, that's what it means for me.

Me: Me too.

Burk: Good.

Burk: Gram says hello.

Me: Tell her hello from me.

Burk: She just got home from the rehab center. Gramps was moved and has situated well. He starts therapy tomorrow and is determined to be home by Christmas.

Me: He's one of the strongest men I know, and if anyone can do it, it's him.

Burk: Agreed. I'm gonna go visit him Tuesday. They gave me the day off, so I asked Gram about it. She said he's gonna be thrilled to see me. Honestly, I'm a little nervous.

Me: I get it. If I were in your shoes, I'd probably be nervous too, but you shouldn't be. His anger was at your dad, not you. I'm sure he regrets what transpired and the fact he distanced himself from you.

Burk: That's what Gram says. I know you're both right, but still. I haven't seen him in about fifteen years.

Me: You're going to reconnect like no time has passed. Just like you did with Gram.

I yawn, watching my phone for a reply to my latest message and glancing up at the top corner of the screen. Holy shit, it's after eleven. We've been talking for two and a half hours when it feels like fifteen minutes.

Burk: I just noticed the time.

Me: Me too. I should try to sleep.

Burk: I'm so sorry. I feel like an asshole for keeping you up so late.

Me: Please don't. I could have signed off at any point. I didn't realize it had gotten so late either.

Burk: Still, I feel bad. 4 a.m. is gonna come early.

I can't help but smile, feeling a little giddy.

Me: It will, but also...worth it. I've enjoyed talking to you.

Burk: Same, Easy-Bake. Same. Good night. Sweet dreams.

Me: Night, Burkey Turkey.

I replace my phone on the charger and curl into my pillow. I'm still smiling, unable to stop. Why? Not just because I spent hours chatting with Burk—and of course, stealing a few kisses. And there wasn't even any mistletoe. It's because I know my dreams will in fact be sweet. They'll be filled with thoughts of him, and most likely his amazing kisses.

Who would have thought little Burk Whitman would have grown up to be so dang gorgeous and such a good kisser? The fourteen-year-old girl in me wouldn't have dreamed about kissing her oldest friend. But the twenty-nine-year-old woman? Oh, she's definitely dreaming about it and will be praying for more.

More of his kisses are now at the top of my Christmas wishlist.

That's exactly what I think about as I drift off to sleep.

"Fourteen dollars and seventy cents," I tell my old kindergarten teacher.

"Keep the change, dear," she replies with a familiar smile.

Taking the bills, I complete the transaction in the register, drop the change into the tip jar, and turn to finish her order. I make her a cinnamon dolce latte, and a regular coffee with cream and sugar, and place a cinnamon roll with two forks on the counter. Her husband is waiting at one of the bistro tables, his walker beside where he sits.

"Here ya go, Mrs. Emerson," I state, grabbing a tray and setting her two steaming cups of Joe and the cinnamon roll on top so she can carry it easier.

"Oh, thank you, Joy. And you know, you can call me Evangeline now."

"I do know," I tell her. What I don't say is that it feels disrespectful to do that, so I'll continue to call her Mrs. Emerson.

The woman who is almost twenty-five years older than she was when she taught me in class grabs the tray. "Your holiday decorations always look so spectacular."

"Thank you. It's my favorite holiday to decorate for," I tell her unnecessarily. Anyone from here knows I go all-out when it comes to Christmas decorations. My goal each year is to bring the magic of the season into my business. I want it to feel like my bakery was plucked right out of the North Pole.

"It shows. It's a wonderland of comfort and warmth in here. And the freshly baked goods surely help," she adds with a smile and a wink before turning to join her husband.

I look up and smile as the bell chimes, announcing another customer. It's almost nine o'clock, a little after the early morning work crowd rush.

"Please tell me you have one of those spiced cherry turnovers left," my sister states as she makes a beeline to the counter. "And a very large, very caffeinated beverage. I'm not picky. Just something big and with a kick. Maybe a double shot of—" she adds, a yawn interrupting her words.

"Why are you so tired?" I ask, yawning the moment she does. They're contagious.

"Biggie was trying to impregnate Miss Snowflake all night. Like *allllll* night, Joy. I don't know how in the world he was able to...you know. Because, *allllll* night!"

I can't help but giggle. "But you had them fixed," I remind her, working my magic at the coffee machine as I prepare her a gingerbread mocha.

"Don't I know, but that's not stopping him. He's insatiable," she grumbles, reaching for the drink before I even have a chance to place it on the counter. "Oh my God, this is like heaven in a cup."

"Thanks," I reply, pulling one of the turnovers out of the case. I make sure to grab the one with the most gooey drizzle on top. "Here."

"You're saving my life, and my sanity," she replies, taking the fork and diving right into her breakfast treat. I yawn a second time since her arrival, and she clearly notices. "Why are you so tired?"

I clear my throat and reach for the cleaning rag, wiping down the counter. "Umm, well, I was talking to someone later than normal."

Her eyebrows shoot upward. "Would this *someone* happen to be Burk Whitman?"

I toss the rag in the sink and prop my hip against the counter. "Maybe."

She squeals, grabs her goodies, and practically runs around the counter. "Tell me everything."

"Hey, Eve," Jan greets, coming out of the kitchen with a tray of cookies.

"Hi, Jan."

"Jan, I'm gonna take a quick five minutes with Eve," I tell the woman who has worked beside me at the bakery since it opened.

"Take your time," she states, rearranging the display case as she adds the freshly baked cookies I made a bit ago.

We pick a table the farthest from customers and sit. "Spill," my sister insists, diving back into her turnover.

"He came over for dinner, helped me decorate my tree, and...he kissed me," I whisper, feeling a ripple of warmth rush through my veins at the memory.

"Of course he did," she murmurs, reaching for her mocha and taking a sip. "And?"

I glance around quickly, my heart fluttering in my chest. "Amazing."

"Whoop!" she cheers. "Isn't it the best feeling? Like every other kiss before you find 'the one' doesn't even compare?"

"The one? Hold your horses, John Wayne. You're putting the cart before the horse."

My sister giggles. "That was a lot of western references in a very short period of time."

"Because you are jumping the gun," I reply, wishing I had grabbed a sweet treat for myself. If I have to talk about kissing Burk and what it means, I definitely require sugar.

"Maybe," she replies casually with a shrug. "Anyway, so he kissed you—"

"Twice," I interrupt, my foot tapping on the floor.

"Nice. Okay, so he kissed you *twice*, and then what?"

"Well, nothing. I mean, after he left, we texted until after eleven something last night, and we have plans to go to the festival this weekend together."

"Aww, that's sweet, but there's nothing romantic about spending the evening surrounded by sugared-up residents of the people of this town."

"Didn't you and John basically have a first date at the festival?"

She waves off my comment. "Totally different."

I bark out a laugh. "Right," I reply, not believing her for a second. "The difference is you and John were meant for each other. Burk and me, well, we're not."

She watches me intently before asking, "Why do you think that?"

I lift my shoulders in a shrug. "He's leaving, Eve. He's only here until the end of the month. I don't exactly see how this can go anywhere, despite how amazing the kisses were."

Eve sighs. "I see your point." She finishes off her turnover before asking, "So what will you do?"

"I guess I'll enjoy my time with my old friend while I can," I reply, knowing there's no reason to get too worked up over it. It's not like this is a relationship.

"And enjoy more kisses," she adds with a smirk.

"Well, duh."

We both chuckle as she sips on her mocha.

"So what about you and John? I think Mom's on Ring Watch."

She rolls her eyes. "She literally checks my finger every morning when I get to work."

I laugh harder. I can definitely see my mom giving her the ring finger check every day. "Not surprising. She's excited for grandkids."

Eve squirms in her seat and casts her eyes down at her drink cup.

"What?"

"What what?" she replies, delaying.

"You got all...twitchy."

"I'm not twitchy," she denies.

"Okay, whatever, twitcher."

She awkwardly chuckles and shakes her head. "Okay, fine. Don't say anything though because it's just talk, all right?"

I nod, anxious to hear what she has to say, and sit up a little taller in my seat.

My sister leans forward and whispers, "We're talking about kids."

"Really? I'll be the bestest auntie ever," I reply eagerly, already thinking about the playdates and the ice cream and the snuggles. Not to mention the overflowing Christmas tree at the holidays.

"You will be," she confirms with a gentle grin. "It might be sooner than expected too."

My mouth drops open and I whisper-yell, "What?!"

She glances around. "I'm not. I mean, I don't think I am. We talked about it a couple weeks ago, and well, we decided we wanted to try right away."

"So, Biggie and Miss Snowflake aren't the only ones getting it on at that house," I tease, watching as my sister yawns and pulls a disgusted face.

"The difference is cats are...loud. And it's not for pleasure, if you know what I mean."

I do, and I'm sorry I said something, honestly.

"Anyway," I say, trying to stop thinking about cat sex. "So, you're all for putting the cart before the horse, huh?"

"What is with you and these horse references?" she asks, laughing.

I shrug. "I don't know, they're just coming to me."

"Well, if it happens, it does, but..."

That's when it hits me. They aren't exactly trying to get pregnant first. "You're engaged!" I whisper-yell again, this time a touch louder.

Eve's eyes widen as she glances around. "No, not yet, but...well, kinda."

"Explain, because I don't know how you get kinda engaged."

"Well, we want to get married at Christmastime because that's when we reconnected, and it's our favorite holiday," she confides.

"Oh my gosh, that'll be so great. And now is the time to start getting stuff because the closer you get to Christmas, the bigger discounts they offer," I state, recalling when I first started purchasing decorations for my tree and the business, I got a lot of it right before or after the big holiday. It's always on clearance to get rid of it and make room for new merchandise. "And a whole year of planning! I'm so excited," I bellow.

She just stares at me. "Not next Christmas, Joy."

"Holy mistletoe, Eve. You're getting married in two and a half weeks!" I proclaim, forgetting to use my indoor voice.

Fortunately, there're only two tables occupied in the bakery and both seem engrossed with those in their party at the time of my outburst.

"Thanks," she mutters.

Covering my mouth with my hand, I mutter a soft, "Sorry."

She waves off my apology. "It's fine. Everyone's gonna know pretty soon anyway. John is meeting with Dad today to ask his permission."

"And what if Dad doesn't give it?" I ask, even though I know he will. My parents love John. He's already been a part of our family for the last year, and they'd never deny my sister the happiness she's found with her first love.

"Do you think he will?" she asks, suddenly worried about the conversation happening later today.

"Of course he won't. We all love John and want him to become an official part of the family. That includes Dad."

She visibly relaxes before looking up and meeting my gaze. "I know he hasn't officially asked me yet, but...will you be my maid of honor?"

"I'd be so pissed if you didn't ask me," I tell her with a giggle.

"It's going to be a very small affair. Just close family and friends."

I know I'm grinning from ear to ear, but I can't help it. I'm so dang happy for her. "It'll be perfect. And I'll help however I can."

"We really don't need much, but I'd love you to make a small cake or something for us. I know it's your busy season—"

"Say no more. I'll take care of everything."

She relaxes again and takes a sip of her mocha. "Thank you, Joy."

"What are little sisters for?"

"I got the best one," she announces before glancing down at her watch. "I should get going. I was heading to the grocery store when I dropped by."

Standing up, I pull my sister into a warm hug. "I'm so happy for you, big sister."

"Thanks," she replies, returning the gesture and squeezing extra hard. "I love you."

"Love you too. Let me know what else I can help with."

"I will."

"Oh, and tell me every detail after he proposes."

She grins like a love-sick teenager. "I will." She tosses her cup and the paper plate that once contained her turnover into the trash can. "Talk soon," she adds, moving toward the door and stepping outside.

I watch as she pulls a stocking cap out of her pocket and slips it on her head. There's no missing the smile etched across her lips as she makes her way to where her vehicle is parked.

My sister's going to get married.

Soon.

And I couldn't be happier for her.

A Christmas wedding is the dream.

With a little extra bounce in my step, I take in the sparkling holiday lights on my tree, start humming "The Wedding March," and get back to work.

Chapter Ten

Burk

"Burk, what's your location?"

I pull the walkie-talkie from the clip and bring it to my mouth, answering my cousin's question. "Wrapping a tree and then heading to the front."

"Ten-four. There's a pretty woman up here to see you." There's no missing the smile in Klint's voice as he replies.

"Be there in a second."

A pretty woman, huh? That can only be one person, and even though I try not to check my watch, I do it anyway. The bakery is closed, but she usually uses the rest of her afternoon to prep for the next day.

So why is she here?

"All set," I tell the older couple as I place the smaller tree onto the sled and make sure all the supplies to cut down and wrap the tree are returned to the crate.

The couple, transplants to Snowflake Falls about five or six years ago, chats as we head back to the front area. As we had made our way into the tree farm, they had explained how they relocated to town because they had both retired and wanted out of the city. They chose Snowflake Falls for its charming small-town feel and friendly vibe and are happy with their move. Their kids and grandkids still live in Aurora, but they come to visit as often as they can.

As I approach the pay hut, I instantly take notice of the woman standing there. It's exactly who I thought—and hoped—it would be, and now that I've laid eyes on Joy, there's a little extra spring in my step as I head her way.

"All right, Mr. and Mrs. Gleason," I start, stepping up to the window in the hut and handing a ticket over to my uncle. "Karl will get you taken care of here, and then we'll get you loaded up."

Karl waves his hand. "I'll load them. Go ahead and visit with your friend," he says, flashing a knowing smile.

I nod and turn my attention to Joy. "Hey."

"Hi," she replies, her green eyes twinkling like Christmas lights as she bounces on her toes. "Sorry to just drop by like this."

I pull off my thick work gloves and nod my head toward the concession stand. "You're fine. Everything okay?" I ask as she falls in line beside me.

"Everything is...perfect." She's smiling so brightly it makes her entire face seem more alive than ever before. "I just got the best news, and I wanted to share it with someone."

I nod. "Let's grab a hot cocoa and we can sit for a few minutes."

She agrees easily and we approach the stand. "Two cocoas, please, Gretchen," I request, pulling my wallet from my back pocket. "Anything else?" I ask, turning toward Joy.

"Oh, no thank you," she replies, offering my cousin's wife a grin.

"Put your money away," Gretchen tells me as she goes about making our cocoas. I know she'll refuse to take any cash I try to give her, so I place it in the tip jar instead. No point in arguing with the woman. She'll still refuse my payment.

"Here ya go. Enjoy," she urges with a big, knowing grin. I know I'll be asked a thousand questions later, first chance she gets.

We each take a cup of cocoa, and with my other hand, I gently lead her toward one of the picnic tables nearby. As soon as we're seated across from each other, she blurts out, "Eve and John are engaged!"

I can't help but return her excitement, smiling widely myself as she practically vibrates off the bench. "Yeah? That's great."

She nods before taking a slight sip of the hot liquid. "He was super sneaky about it too. She came in this morning and told me he was going to ask Dad's permission. Well, apparently, he had already done that, so when he sent her off to the grocery store, he set up his house for a big proposal. He had extra twinkle lights and red roses everywhere. He even tied the ring to Miss Snowflake's collar."

"And Miss Snowflake is..."

"Her cat. He has a cat too, Biggie, who loves to fornicate with her."

If I had cocoa in my mouth, it would have gone flying at that exact moment. "What?" I ask, choking on air instead.

She nods. "True story. They're like...bunnies. Or something. Anyway, they don't even officially live together yet. They both still have their own places next door to each other, and they switch back and forth between them, so I imagine they'll be moving in together sooner rather than later."

"Well, an engagement gives them time, right?"

She just grins at my question. "You'd think, but no. They're getting married on Christmas."

"*This* Christmas?" My mouth drops open in shock. That's less than three weeks away.

"Yep, this Christmas." She takes a quick drink of her chocolatey cocoa before adding, "It's going to be very small and intimate. She wants to get married in the old stone church at the edge of town."

I remember that old building. It's situated inside the cemetery and features big windows and a rustic fireplace. "I didn't even realize they did weddings there."

"Well, they don't do many because it's so small. Plus, there's no air and the only heat comes from the fireplace."

I've never been inside the building, but we'd ride bikes out there when we were younger. I recall peeking inside the windows and seeing the small wooden pews and the stone fireplace altar. "Sounds perfect, actually."

"Doesn't it?" Joy beams with delight. "She wants to do the ceremony around seven so it's completely dark outside. The only light inside will be candles and the fireplace. It's going to be rustic, romantic, and completely perfect."

"Well, I'm happy for them. Extend my congratulations for me."

"I will." She takes another sip. "Not only do I get to serve as her maid of honor, but I get to make the cake too. And we're going dress shopping Sunday afternoon. She doesn't want anything fancy and says she's fine with off the rack. There's a boutique in Edgemere that's open on Sundays through the holidays, so we're going there to find dresses. She told me I can pick whatever I wanted, but since it's a Christmas wedding, I'm hoping to find something in a deep green or red, you know?"

I nod, the smile never slipping from my face.

"I'm sorry," she murmurs, covering her mouth with her gloved hand. "I've been droning on and on since we sat down."

"It's fine. You're excited, I can tell."

"I am," she confirms. "I'm just, well, I'm happy for her. After everything that happened with Andrew, I want her to have every ounce of happiness she can get."

My own smile is genuine and easy, because I do understand. I want that for Eve, but also for Joy. I want her to have everything she can get out of this life, including love. After hearing about that asshole Eli cheating on her, I want it even more for her.

And a part of me longs to be the one to give it to her...

But that's not in the cards. After Christmas, I'll be heading back to South Carolina, back to my old life. I have a job, my family, and friends there.

But you have those things here too...

"Anyway, I was just so excited after work when she called me, I had to tell someone. And it's not like I'm telling her secret before she has a chance to, because it's you. I tell you everything," she states, as if no time has passed since that statement was true. When we were younger, we'd tell each other everything, as best friends would do.

I find myself reaching out and covering her gloved hand with my bare one. Even though the air is crisp and cold, I can feel the heat from her skin through the wool material. We both take a drink, neither moving our hands. It's intimate, and maybe I shouldn't do it right here in the middle of my family's tree farm—a family who is no doubt watching us like hawks from cover somewhere.

"So, I have one more question for you," she asks, her cheeks turning a deeper shade of pink. Something tells me it's not from the cold air either.

"Shoot."

"Would you go with me? To their wedding?"

"Like a—"

"Date," she blurts out, cutting me off. "Yes, will you be my date for my sister's wedding?"

"I'd love to."

The apples of her cheeks redden even more as she grins and glances down. "I know it's Christmas and all, but it shouldn't take too long. Wedding at seven and then we're having cake and whatnot afterward at my parents' house."

"I'd be honored to escort you, Easy-Bake."

"Okay," she replies, shifting in her seat. "Good. Great."

Her nervousness is adorable as fuck.

"Is there a dress code for guests?" I ask, thinking about what I brought with me. I don't have a suit, but I'd happily go purchase one if needed.

"The groom is going to wear jeans with a sport coat, and she wants all guests to be comfortable. Jeans and a button-down or sweater would be fine."

"No ugly Christmas sweater?" I joke.

"Don't give her any ideas!" she bellows with a laugh.

"I have nice jeans and a button-down with me. I'm sure I can borrow a tie from Gramps or Klint."

She nods and reaches for her cup once more. We spend the next ten minutes chatting and enjoying our cocoa, and by the time the cups are empty, I know I need to get back to work. My fifteen-minute break is up.

"Thanks for letting me interrupt your workday," she says, standing up and taking my empty cup to toss in the nearby trash can.

"Anytime. As long as I'm not super busy, I'll take as much time as I can to visit."

Taking her hand, I walk her to the lot where her car is parked. When we reach the driver's door, I lean in and brush my lips across hers. I don't look around to see if anyone is nearby or watching. I don't care. All I want is to steal a quick kiss before I get back to work.

Mission accomplished.

"What's this I hear about you kissing on the Campbell girl in the parking lot?"

I stop in my tracks the moment her words reach my ears. "You spying on me?" I tease, even though I'm sure it wasn't Gram.

She just shrugs and continues to stir the amazing-smelling pot on the stove. "It doesn't matter how I found out, just that I did."

I bark out a laugh. "Was it Klint or Gretchen?"

"I'll never tell," she insists, smiling from ear to ear. "I'm glad you're here. Dinner's about ready."

"What did you make?" I ask, heading in her direction to take a peek.

"White chicken chili."

My stomach growls with no shame. I haven't even been here a week yet, and already my pants are getting a little snug. "Sounds like heaven," I tell her, grabbing two bowls out of the cabinet and placing them on the counter.

"Grab the sour cream and taco cheese out of the fridge," she tells me as she pulls a bag of tortilla strips from the pantry.

She scoops me a hearty bowl of her white chicken chili and hands it over before making her own bowl. I add a bit of shredded taco cheese, a dollop of sour cream, and a handful of the tortilla strips before taking my dinner to the bar. Gram hasn't sat at the dining room table since Gramps had his medical emergency, so I make sure to sit where I know she'll be comfortable.

"I need a favor," she says after taking her first bite.

"Shoot." I'm trying not to inhale my food, but it's damn good.

"There's some stuff I'd like your help with moving. I know you're busy with work—and your friend, Joy—but I'm hoping you can do something for me. It won't take too long. I could ask Klint to do it, but he's at the other house, and—"

"Say no more. I'd be happy to do whatever you need, Gram."

She smiles softly, scooping up another bite. "There's some wood I'd like to have moved and sorted in the shed. Some of it might be good yet, but I don't know. I want to get it all cleaned up before Gramps gets home and ensure there's a clean walkway through the shop. It'd be just my luck he'd trip over something in the way and break his dang hip."

I nod in understanding. "I can do that. How about tomorrow after I get back from visiting him?"

"There's no rush, dear. It's not like Gramps is coming home in the next day or two."

"Still. I'll get it done as quickly as I can. Anything else in there you want me to do?" I ask, trying to remember what's in that old shed. I recall it being there, a steel building just behind the garage, but I don't really remember much about it. It was always locked, and Gramps said it was his man cave. He'd go in and tinker or do small projects when work wasn't too busy. Since he spent so much of his time tending to the farm, I'm not sure when he actually used that space.

"I don't think so. I can go in and sweep and tidy up a bit."

"I'll do it," I volunteer, even though I don't know what I'm getting into. I do know my Gramps keeps things pretty organized and clean. The barn and outbuildings for the farm are in good working order, and the house has been well maintained. I can't see a big mess or a clusterfuck of crap in his shed.

"Thank you, Burk," she replies with a gentle smile, reaching over and giving my hand a squeeze. "Gramps knows you're coming tomorrow," she states, and when I meet her gaze she adds, "He's looking forward to your visit."

I swallow hard and nod. "I am too."

"Just don't sneak him in those Christmas tree Little Debbie cakes he likes. They're trying to watch his sugar and cholesterol and have told him to keep his snacking to a minimum."

I snort a laugh. "I bet that's going over well," I deadpan, recalling how Gramps always liked his sweets. He was a tall, lean man, but he had the sweetest tooth of anyone I'd known. He always carried candies or chocolates in his coat pockets. Gram would regularly have to check the pockets so they didn't wind up in the washing machine.

"You know him."

I nod, even though I'm not sure that's true. I knew him back when I was a kid, but even those memories have slowly started to fade over time. I knew the man he was, not the man he is now, though, in my heart, something tells me those people are still one and the same. "No worries there, Gram. I'd never sneak him in contraband."

She chuckles and takes another bite of her chili. "Good boy."

"Why anyone would eat those things is beyond me, especially when you have a delicious bakery right here in town. If I were going to slip him something, it'd be the good stuff. Like one of her cinnamon rolls, caramel apple pie bites, or some gingerbread cookies."

Gram just grins at me. "You like her, and I'm not talking about reconnecting the friendship you used to share."

I clear my throat and decide to speak honestly. "I wouldn't have kissed her if I didn't."

She nods, appreciating my response. "I've always liked that girl, and I'm not saying that because her dad works for us. She's got a good head on her shoulders and works hard."

"She does."

"And she's awfully pretty," Gram adds, making me smile.

"That she is."

"Anyway, I'm glad you're enjoying your time here. I sure am loving having you."

My heart gallops in my chest as I long for slivers of the childhood I left behind. "I love being here. I'm sorry I've stayed away so long."

She waves off my apology. "The good news is you're here now, and the door is always open, Burk. We'll do better at visiting you in South Carolina too, but I hope you know you're always welcome here."

"I do," I answer.

"Good. And Gramps is expecting you any time after ten. His physical therapy is at nine, and it takes about an hour. He'll probably be pretty worn out, but he's always up for visitors."

"You're not going?" I ask. I don't know why the thought of being alone with him makes me a bit more nervous. Probably because it's been so damn long since I've seen him, and the last time was when he and my dad were exchanging not-so-pleasant words with each other.

"Oh, I'll drop by for my visit in the afternoon. I want to give you both time to catch up."

I nod in reply, my throat thick. "I'm a bit nervous, Gram."

"Don't be, Burk. What happened back then wasn't about you. It was simply two hardheaded men airing feelings they should have talked about long before. I'm sorry it happened. I'm even more sorry I didn't do more to try to fix it."

I give Gram a gentle smile and reach across the table for her hand, offering a squeeze. "We can't change that. We can only move forward."

She moves her hand to cover my own and pats it. "Absolutely. Now, let's eat before it gets cold. Then, perhaps you have time to call that pretty girl of yours before she goes to bed."

With a wink, she returns her focus on eating her dinner, and I do the same.

Only my mind is locked on a certain pretty girl. The one who consumes all my thoughts, day and night. The one I want to steal kisses from every chance I get.

The one who makes my heart feel happier than ever before

Chapter Eleven

Joy

Eve: I have an opening this afternoon.

Me: I'll take it!

Eve: 3 p.m. I have time for color and cut.

Me: Perfect, thank you!

I smile as I slip my cell phone back into my pocket and finish icing cupcakes for the display case. After chatting with my sister earlier when she and John stopped for their caffeine fix, I mentioned wanting to do something different with my hair. She thought she'd have time today to work me in, and I'm so happy to hear she can.

I don't know what I want to do exactly. I have to leave it long enough to pull back when baking, but I think I want to add bangs. Not like when we were in high school and you just took a pair of scissors to them and regretted it later. Nothing blunt or harsh. I'm thinking swooping bangs across my face I can sweep to the side. Maybe I'll try to find a picture I can show Eve.

The bell chimes above the door, and I keep working, knowing Jan will handle the arriving customers. I got dang lucky when she walked in to be interviewed right before I opened. I wasn't sure if I would be able to swing employees, especially at first, but she's been nothing but a godsend. Not only is she friendly and excellent at customer service, but she quickly picked up on what it would take to be a barista and make the specialty drinks we serve. Our menu isn't as extensive as those chain coffee shops, but we have a decent selection to pair with whatever sweet treat you're craving.

"Joy, you have a visitor."

I look to the front of the bakery, and spot Burk standing at the counter. Unable to fight a smile, I flash one at his sudden appearance and wave him back. "What are you doing here?" I ask, knowing he's on his way to visit his grandpa.

"I thought I'd stop by and grab something for Gramps. You know how he is with his sweet tooth," he says as he makes his way to where I stand.

"I just put some traditional decorated sugar cookies in the display case," I tell him, setting my piping bag down on the workstation.

"I did see those, but what are these?" he asks, moving to stand beside me. I feel the heat of his body, even though we're not touching, and catch the woodsy scent of his soap on his skin. He smells better than all the sugar cookies in the world.

Clearing my throat, I glance down at the cupcakes. "Cherry chip cupcakes with buttercream Christmas trees on top," I tell him, loving how cute the mountain of frosting looks on top of the small piece of cake.

"Oh, I think he'd love one of those," Burk agrees, practically licking his lips.

A giggle slips from my lips as I turn to grab a small pastry box. "Gramps would love one or Burk would love one?"

"Yes."

I take a quick second to assemble the box before adding, "Well, I'll send you with two so you can enjoy them together."

"Thanks," he says, propping a hip against the counter and watching me. "I'll probably add a few cookies too."

"Of course."

"Gram said not to buy him those processed Christmas tree cakes he loves so much, but why would I do that when he can have a delicious homemade treat instead?"

I stick out my tongue. "Those things taste like wax. I used to love them when I was little, but now that I'm older and make my own treats, I can't even stomach eating them."

"I think you've ruined me too, Easy-Bake," he states, taking the small box that holds two cupcakes perfectly.

"That just means when you need a sweet fix, you have to come here to get it," I tease, realizing immediately my mistake. Burk's only here for a few more weeks, and then he'll be back home in South

Carolina. Him dropping by the bakery will end, and I don't like the way my stomach—and my heart—feel at that thought.

He just grins back at me and doesn't dwell on the fact his time here has an expiration date. "So," he starts, rocking back on his heels, "I'm nervous."

"Why?"

"Because I haven't seen him in fifteen years."

"But he's so excited you're coming to visit. Your gram told my dad that. He wants to mend your relationship."

He nods. "I know. She basically told me the same thing last night at dinner, but, I guess, what if we don't really have anything in common? What if it's just awkward and uncomfortable?"

"Well, then you leave," I tell him bluntly. "But honestly, I don't think it's going to be. You're a lot more like your grandpa than you think. You're both hard workers and love to do things with your hands. Once that initial tension is broken, I truly believe you're going to fall into easy conversation, and it won't feel like the last fifteen years have passed at all."

He gives a grateful look, as if I said exactly what he needed to hear. I know he's anxious to see his grandpa, and I don't blame him. It's been a lot of years. But I believe wholeheartedly that everything will be just fine.

"Oh, I talked to my uncle about leaving early Saturday. I'm off at four, so I'll run up to the house and shower and change. I should be to your place around five."

"Okay, great. Do you have skates?"

He groans and shakes his head. "I knew you were going to ask that, and no. I'll have to rent them."

"But you *will* skate with me, right?"

"I will. I haven't done it since I lived here, and something tells me it's not quite like riding a bike. Especially since I wasn't that good at it the first time around."

I just beam up at him with excitement. "I can't wait. Eve skates with me but complains the whole time. She'd much rather ride all the spinny carnival rides than go ice skating."

"Well, no worries, Easy-Bake. We have a date. Maybe if I slip and fall every four minutes you'll take mercy on me and give me a good rubdown," he replies jovially, but then sobers.

I can tell the moment his words infiltrate his brain, and he catches his innuendo. Of course, my own brain has zeroed in on his words, and I can't help but think about giving him a good *rubdown* after skating. In my mind, we're both naked—or well on our way to being—when it happens.

"Anyway," he mutters, a faint blush on his cheeks. "I should get on the road."

"Let me know how it goes," I start before adding, "if you want."

He flashes a quick grin. "I want. I'll chat with you later," he says, picking up the two cupcakes and adding, "Thanks for these."

"You're welcome."

"I'm gonna stop up front and grab a few cookies to go with them. That'll be sure to give him a sugar rush before I leave."

"Mmmm, I love a good sugar rush," I tell him.

He chuckles. "I bet you do." Then, he leans in and brushes his lips across mine. "If that's the kind of sugar you're offering, I do enjoy a good sugar rush myself."

My giggle comes out all giddy, and I practically swoon at his comment. And the kiss.

I watch as he walks around the counter and picks out a few of the holiday-themed sugar cookies. Jan bags them up and gives him a total. After he pays, he looks back into the kitchen and waves. I return the gesture and watch as he exits the building, his jeans accentuating what little bit of his ass I can see beneath his coat.

Turning my attention back to the cupcakes, I let my fingers brush across my lips. The kiss was chaste, too quick for my liking, but it still packed a punch. It does every single time our lips connect.

Kissing him has become my sugar rush.

"I have an idea," my sister says as soon as I sit in her chair.

A single eyebrow shoots upward. "An idea?"

Eve nods eagerly. "It's a little different, but I think it's going to look so amazing on you."

"Are you going to tell me what it is?" I ask, somewhat hesitantly.

My sister continues to stare at me through the mirror. "I don't want to, but I will, because if you hated it, I'd feel awful. Not that I think you wouldn't like it, because I think you totally will. It's a slightly different style and a fresh color."

"Okay," I reply with a casual shrug. "I trust you."

She pulls out her phone and cues up a photo. "This is the cut," she replies, handing over the device. "It's an angled lob, and it would work well with your oval face."

"I like it," I tell her, realizing instantly that I do. It's shorter than I was thinking, but it's super cute with longer hair in the front and shorter hair in the back.

"And I thought maybe we could try this…" She pulls up another photo on her phone and shows me the screen.

"Oh."

"It's darker than we normally do, but I think this color of chestnut would really complement the cut."

She's right, it's darker and provides more all-over coverage. Usually, I just use highlights or lowlights to give my dark-blond hair depth, but this would change my color entirely.

I flip back and forth between the cut and the color a few more times before lifting my head and meeting her gaze. "Let's do it."

"Really?" she asks, her green eyes, the same color as my own, sparkling.

"Yep."

"If you hate the darker color, we can always fix it," she tells me, grabbing the cape and wrapping it around my neck.

"I'm not going to hate it," I reassure.

"What did she think?" Mom comes up front after mixing her own client's color in the back room.

"We're doing it," Eve announces, earning a big smile from our mom.

"That style is so popular right now, and I agree that it'll look great on you," Mom says, pulling a stack of foil squares off her cart.

"And I think it'll still be long enough to pull back while I'm at the bakery," I add, hoping that's true.

Looking at Eve in the mirror, she gives me a knowing nod. "Yep, I'll make sure you can still pull it back."

I relax in the chair as she preps for my color. It's been a while since she's colored my whole head like this. The one and only time I thought I wanted to be blonder happened back when she was in her early days of beauty school. She colored me with something closer to a platinum blonde, and it wasn't a good look for me. Since then, we've stuck with highlights and lowlights in shades only slightly lighter and darker than my natural color, which suits me just fine.

Eve gets to work on my hair, adding the color methodically. I watch her as she concentrates on her task, Mom doing the same at her chair. "How are the wedding plans coming along?" I ask, even though it's only been a day. My sister got a lot done yesterday, including setting up the venue for the ceremony and finding a boutique open on Sundays so we can shop for dresses.

"I'm meeting with Debi at the flower shop on Thursday. She's agreed to make a couple of small bouquets and boutonnieres for me. Plus, there's a candlelight Christmas Eve service the night before, and the pastor told me the altar arrangements will still be there so we can just use those."

"I still love the Christmas theme," I tell her. "It's very fitting for you."

"I agree," she practically sways with giddiness. "It's my absolute favorite holiday, and I truly want something simple, yet magical. I know it's a huge request, asking people to give up part of their holiday, but—"

"Everyone will be thrilled to share this with you. And your wedding isn't until later in the day, so no one is really losing much. Plus, this is special, and anyone who knows and loves you will be honored to be there."

She grins at me through the mirror. "Our guest list is about twenty people."

"And that'll be absolutely perfect."

She nods eagerly. "I think so too. And the church is so small. We wouldn't be able to pack many more in there."

"Intimate is the word I'm using," she replies, continuing to work.

"That's exactly it. It's going to be such a beautiful, intimate night. I can't wait to share it with you," I state, as something else hits me. "Oh, I asked Burk to be my plus one. I hope that's okay."

Her smile is slow as she pauses what she's doing and meets my gaze through the mirror. "Of course it is."

Starting to feel a little uncomfortable for not asking her about bringing a date first, I reply, "If that makes it too many people, or you'd rather it just be immediate family and close friends, I'd understand."

She waves her latex glove-covered hand at me. "Oh, stop it. Of course you can bring a date. Bonus points that it's Burk." She waggles her eyebrows suggestively at me before leaning in so Mom and her client can't overhear. "Maybe you'll get more than just some kisses under your tree this year."

My eyes widen at her brazen statement. Not because I haven't thought that myself, but simply because she did. "Stop it," I whisper.

Eve just grins a knowing, naughty little smile. "I'm willing to bet it'll happen before Christmas."

Now my cheeks flush a dark shade of red.

"What'll happen before Christmas?" Mom asks from her station.

"Nothing," I insist at the same time Eve says, "Joy's got the hots for her best friend, and they're going to the festival this weekend together."

My mouth drops open at her announcement.

"Oh, I love that!" Mom declares. "You two were thick as thieves when you were little. I love the fact you've reconnected, and it appears romantic this time around."

"You do?" I find myself asking.

"Of course," she replies with a supportive-laced smile. "He's such a nice young man. Much better than the last jerk."

I can't help but bark out a laugh at her mention of Eli.

"I agree," Eleanor Davis says from Mom's chair.

"Okay, next subject," I encourage, wanting to move this conversation away from Burk and me. It's one thing to talk about it with my sister, but another thing entirely to add in my mom and her client.

Two hours later, I'm turned away from the mirror as my sister finishes styling my hair. It already feels so different, so much lighter, and I can't wait to see how it's turned out. The color is definitely a touch darker than I would have picked, but I don't hate it. In fact, it's quickly growing on me.

"Are you ready?" Eve asks, taking off the cape and preparing to spin me around for the big reveal.

"As I'll ever be."

She gently spins the chair, giving me my first glimpse of my new haircut and color together. "Oh my Christmas bells," I whisper, making everyone laugh.

"Christmas bells are good, right?" Mom asks, coming over to the chair I'm sitting in.

A few seconds later, Roxie, the other stylist, joins us. "Oh my gosh, you look so gorgeous, Joy. Not that you didn't before but that color and cut is chef's kiss." She makes the gesture by bringing her fingertips to her lips and kissing.

I stare at my hair, a giddy feeling erupting in my gut. "I love it."

"I'm so glad," Eve says, lowering the chair so I can get up. "And it'll be super easy to maintain. Plus, I left it a touch long all the way around to ensure you can pull it up while working."

I nod, my eyes glued to the light brown locks. It's spectacular, and I'm so glad I let her do it.

After I pay for my services and leave a healthy tip, I give hugs to both my mom and sister and make my way next door. The bakery is clean, but I still have a little prep work to do for tomorrow. Plus, I want to nail down exactly what sweet treats and drink selections I'm going to offer Friday night. I'll be open from five to seven with another limited menu option for those attending the festival, and I have a few ideas, but I need to ensure I have the ingredients.

As I unlock the door and step inside the bakery, I pull out my phone and smile when I see a message from Burk.

> **Burk:** Hope your day is going well. I'm still visiting Gramps. You were right. This is just what I needed. I'm having a great time.

> **Me:** I knew it! I'm happy you're reconnecting with him. Enjoy your visit.

He replies almost instantly with a smiley face emoji that mirrors my own grin as I slip the device back into my pocket, remove my coat, and flip on the lights in my kitchen. Pushing thoughts of Burk aside is hard, but I somehow manage while I finalize my plan for Friday night.

Of course, as soon as I'm finished, Burk is right back in the forefront of my brain.

And I don't hate it.

Thinking about him has quickly become one of my favorite pastimes.

Chapter Twelve

Burk

"I'm glad you came," Gramps states as I prepare to leave.

I've been here all day, or at least since about ten thirty, and now it's almost completely dark outside when I glance out the window. We had lunch together in the private dining room for families and then came back to his room, where we've been catching up all afternoon. We shared the cupcakes for an afternoon snack, and I helped him hide the sugar cookies in his nightstand drawer.

Now, it's close to dinnertime and Gram is on her way. Both offered for me to stay and eat with them, but I want to give them a little time together. I know Gram stayed away longer than normal so Gramps and I could visit, and while I've loved spending that time with him, I really should get back.

Plus, since I have the whole day off, I plan to move the piles of wood Gram asked me to move to clean up the shed for when he comes home.

"I am too." With my throat suddenly thick with emotion, I add, "I'm sorry I've stayed away so long."

His eyes turn misty as he stares up at me from his chair. "That's my fault, Burk. I shouldn't have let emotions get in the way of family. I shouldn't have let it continue so long." He exhales and closes his eyes for a brief moment. "I'm stubborn. All of us Whitman men are. I had a vision of what the family farm would be, and when your dad came to me and said he didn't want to be a part of it anymore, I didn't take it well. I should have listened better. I regret it. All of it."

I nod, thinking about how alike my dad and his dad are. Both are stubborn like mules, and while I don't know if their relationship is repairable, I do know I can do my part in fixing the one I have with my grandparents. "I promise not to let the past have any more hold on my future."

He gives me a sad smile. "You were young, boy, and I should have made a bigger effort. Even if I was mad at your dad, I shouldn't have let it affect our relationship."

"It's okay," I assure, but he quickly chimes back in.

"No, it's not, but I'll do better. Gram loves having you here. I wish I were home so I could be there and work beside you, but it's not in the cards yet. But I'm gonna put in the work. My goal is to be home for Christmas, and I'll do my damnedest to make it happen."

My heart is practically tap dancing in my chest with giddiness. "That would be pretty great, but even if you're not out of here yet, I'm sure we'll all come see you here."

He smiles, the right side of his face not quite catching up to the left yet. The stroke has affected the left side of his body, especially his leg and arm. They're both weaker now, which is why the rehab program here is necessary. Fortunately, it didn't affect his speech much, which would have created another layer of difficulty to his therapy program.

"Well, you have that wedding to go to that day," Gramps announces, catching me off guard.

I'm surprised he's heard about that, considering Joy just asked me to go yesterday and I haven't told anyone yet. But that's Snowflake Falls for you. It's a small town where everyone knows your business.

"I do," I confirm.

"I also hear you're spending some time with Joy." His statement is laced with humor but not like he's laughing at me. It's more the fact he knows and is ready for me to dispute it.

"I am," I answer.

"She's a good egg."

"She is," I agree.

"Well, enjoy your time with her."

I can't help but smile. "I will."

"All right, well get out of here. I'm sure you have better things to do than hang with me all day," he insists, shifting in his chair as best he can, considering his right-side weakness.

"Gram should be here shortly," I reply, just as the door pushes open.

"I'm here now," she announces, stepping into the room and giving us both a wide grin. She walks over to set her purse on the bed before bending down and giving Gramps a kiss. "Have you been behaving?" she asks, a knowing glint in her eyes.

"Of course I have!" he insists, his eyes betraying us when he glances toward his nightstand.

Gram catches the movement of his eyes and walks over to open the drawer. Slowly, she turns and pins me with a stern look.

"Get out of my stuff, woman!" Gramps teases, feigning outrage.

"Hey, you told me not to bring him those nasty Christmas tree cakes. I didn't," I reply, crossing my arms over my chest and standing my ground.

Gramps gasps. "Nasty?"

"I never said nasty, even though they're not great, Dale," Gram replies, shutting the drawer and shaking her head. "I suppose if you're going to cheat, it should be with goodies from The Sweet Escape."

"I was supporting a local entrepreneur," I add, fighting a smile.

Gram waves off my comment. "Oh, please. You were just necking with the owner."

Gramps' eyes widen with delight. "Necking? You've been necking?"

"All right, I'm out of here," I state, walking over and placing a kiss on Gram's cheek. "I'll see you back at the house."

"Drive safe, Burk," she replies, giving me a hug.

"I will."

Turning to my grandpa, I reach out my left hand. He reaches with his and tugs, wrapping his good arm around my neck for a hug. His right one moves at a much slower rate, and eventually I feel that hand touch my arm. He gives it a squeeze, but it's still incredibly weak. "Come back soon," he whispers, and I'm man enough to admit, I get a little choked up.

"I will. Promise."

He smiles a crooked smile and releases me. "Next time, I want to hear more about your time with Joy."

I roll my eyes. "Isn't anything private around here?"

He just barks out a laugh. "Not in this town, it isn't."

I wave goodbye to both my grandparents and exit the room, feeling much lighter than I have in a very long time. Reconnecting with my grandparents has been one of the greatest parts of this trip back to Colorado. Doing the same with Joy is also at the top of the list.

Being here feels good, and the thought of heading back to the opposite side of country causes a lump to form in my throat and the knot to tighten in my chest. I like it here. Just like I did growing up. So what now?

Well, now, I'm going to push those thoughts out of my head and do what I came here to do. I'll help my family with the tree farm business during peak season, spending as much time with Joy as I can on the side. What comes next can wait until, well, later.

Tonight, I'm going to go back to the farm and take care of Gramps' shed. I can't wait to see what he's been hiding inside that building.

Holy mistletoe!

I wasn't expecting this.

I stand in the open doorway, staring, my jaw unhinged in complete shock.

"What the hell?" I mutter, stepping inside the shed and closing the door. I find the light switches and bathe the entire space in light.

All I can do is gape.

Gramps has an entire woodworking shop in here, and I had no clue.

Running my hand down my face, I just take in the sight of his space. I don't really remember him being in here, and when he was, I was too busy doing my own thing to worry about what was inside. Now, I wish I would have paid closer attention, maybe spent some time here with him. I've always loved woodworking and have made a career out of it. I learned a lot from my neighbor, but could you imagine if I had also been able to learn from Gramps too?

I notice the pile of wood sitting off to the side. There's a variety of scraps and odds and ends all thrown together. My mind starts to work, as it always does when I see random pieces of wood. What can I make with that?

I shake off the thought, because that's not what I'm here for. I told Gram I'd help get this place ready for Gramps's return, and that's what I'll do.

But first...I take a tour of his shop.

He has everything you need and a handful of wants too. Table saw, band saw, miter saw, wood lathe, and more. Not to mention a wall of hand tools, all in their own spot, and every accessory you can possibly think of.

This place is a replica of my own shop back at home.

I shake my head as I take in the tools, surprised, yet not surprised. Gramps has always been handy around the property, that I remember from when I was younger. So it really doesn't shock me too much that he'd have a hobby where he works with his hands. I guess to discover we have this in common just strikes a chord.

After spending time admiring his shop, I move to the scrap pile of wood and start sorting it. Some of it needs to go straight to the burn pit, as Gram suggested, but there's a few decent pieces here, and my brain instantly starts spinning ideas. I lay the good pieces across the workstation in the middle of the room and check them over.

Then, I get to work.

When I finish, I step back and smile at the multi-bottle wine bottle and glass holder. It's not stained or finished yet, but it's a great, random piece. I didn't use any template, just went with my gut, and that rarely leads me astray.

I leave the piece I made sitting on the table and start sweeping up the wood shavings and tossing the scraps into a bucket. I haul the pieces I'm going to burn outside and place them in the firepit. When I remove the larger scraps, I find a torch lighter sitting on the shelf and bring it along. After all the wood Gram requested I move is out of the building, I light the firepit and step back to watch.

My phone vibrates in my pocket, and I'm instantly hit with a mix of emotions. I'm anxious, hoping it's Joy who's messaging me, and I feel terrible I didn't let her know when I was back from my visit with Gramps.

Joy: I hope you enjoyed your visit. Heading to bed and was wanting to tell you goodnight.

Instead of replying to her text, I hit the phone icon and bring the phone to my ear.

"Hello?" she answers, her smile evident in her voice.

"Hey, beautiful. Hope I'm not waking you up."

Her chuckle comes through the phone line as she replies, "I just sent you a text less than thirty seconds ago."

Grinning from ear to ear, I take a seat on a stump near the firepit. I stare at the glow of the flames as they dance across the dark sky, grateful to be close enough to feel the heat, since I'm not wearing a coat. "I know, but maybe you're the type of person who falls asleep the moment her head hits the pillow," I reason.

"Oh, I assure you, I am not that person. As tired as I am at the end of the day, sometimes it's hard to fall asleep early, especially if the sun is still out in the summer. I like to read to help me fall asleep, but sometimes that can have the opposite effect," she says with a giggle.

"I like quiet. Just me and my fan."

Her gasp echoes through the device in my hand. "A fan? Say it isn't so, Burkey Turkey."

"Oh, it's so, Easy-Bake. A fan is a requirement. I even have a small portable one I travel with."

She snorts. "Of course you do."

"And let me guess, you're always cold and have ten blankets on your bed." I'm totally picturing her lying in bed right now—*naked*, because it's my fantasy—and burrowed in the middle of a mountain of blankets.

"Not quite ten, but I do have two. My favorite Christmas quilt is there, but I also have a really soft fleece blanket I snuggle with, because there's nothing worse than cold sheets."

"I'm surprised you don't have those flannel ones," I say, kicking my feet out in front of me and watching the fire.

"Oh, I do. Lots of them. The ones I have on now are polar bears playing on ice, but sometimes I'm just cold."

"Hmm, so you're saying you need something—or *someone*—to help keep you warm," I reply, my voice dropping low with the innuendo.

She doesn't reply right away, and I start to worry I took it too far, but then she adds, "I do get awfully cold in bed alone. It would be convenient to have something or some*one* to keep me warm."

I'm about to volunteer for the job, but I'm pretty sure she doesn't need me to spell it out for her. She knows I'm interested, or at least I think she does. The last thing I want is her picturing someone else warming her bed.

"Burk?" she asks, interrupting my thoughts.

"Hmm?"

"It's you I see keeping me warm in bed."

A groan slides from my lips and my cock gets hard. When I close my eyes, I picture it perfectly, her naked body lying in the middle of her bed, wrapped in that damn Christmas quilt, and now, it's all I can think of. It consumes me, like the fire dancing in the pit before me. They lick my skin and devour me whole.

"Noted, Joy," I whisper in a voice that doesn't quite sound like mine.

"So…Saturday night, right?"

"Yes, Saturday night," I reply, wishing the week away so we can get to our date.

She yawns through the phone, and I know I should let her get to sleep. "I hope today went well for you," she murmurs.

"It did. I had a good time getting to know him again."

"I was right, huh?"

I chuckle and smile as I reply, "Yeah, Easy-Bake, you were right."

"I'm always right."

Snorting, I retort, "I don't know about that. I recall a certain someone insisting the math test wasn't on the Monday after that zoo field trip, only to find out it was. And do you remember my grade, Joy?"

"Not my fault," she defends.

"Lies. You said it was Tuesday, and in fact, it was not."

"Well, maybe you should have taken your own notes in your assignment book instead of expecting me to do it."

I gasp. "You volunteered! You had that fancy little Trapper Keeper thingy with the stupid cuddly bear and puppy dog on it and insisted it was the best assignment book in the world."

"Oh, it was," she insists. "It was so cool, in fact, those fancy things are making a comeback. I almost bought one the other day."

I bark out a laugh. "For assignment keeping?"

"Yes."

Chuckling, I lean back on the stump and try to get comfortable. "I'd buy you a thousand."

"Well, I don't need a thousand, silly. Only one, but it must have the cuddly bear and puppy on it."

I make a mental note to look for the Trapper Keeper she's referring to next time I go to the big box store. When she yawns a second time, I know I need to let her go. "I enjoy reminiscing with you."

"I enjoy it too." She's silent for several seconds before adding, "I really have missed you, Burk."

"I've missed you too, Joy. Sleep well."

"You too," she replies, her voice soft, her grin evident. "Night."

"Good night," I reply, almost letting a sweetheart slip past my lips. The term of endearment feels natural to want to say, but I stop it before the word is out there. Instead, I listen as she disconnects our call and whisper gently into the night air. "Sweetheart."

As I watch the flames dance, my mind starts to spin with ideas. There are dozens of things I could make for Joy, but only one keeps coming back to the forefront of my mind. I pull out my phone and do a quick search for styles and know I'll jot some design ideas down later on when I get inside.

For now, I'm content to just sit here, watch the fire, and think about the woman who seems to be consuming my every thought, day and night.

She's quickly becoming an obsession.

A beautiful reminder of the life I once had and the one I want moving forward.

Problem is, those two worlds don't meet in the middle.

Chapter Thirteen

Joy

"Are you hungry?" Burk asks as we approach the line of food trucks.

"Starving," I confess. "I didn't get a chance to eat much today. We were really busy. Lots of holiday shoppers out and about."

He nods, placing his hand on my lower back and guiding toward the row of food. Truth is, not only am I ravenous for food, but I'm exhausted to boot. Saturdays are always one of my biggest days, but during the holiday season, it's worse. The sidewalks are filled with shoppers, all doing their part in staying local through the gift-giving season as much as possible.

However, even though I'm dead on my feet, there was no way I was canceling this evening. In fact, from the moment I opened my door and found Burk standing there, I've felt an overwhelming renewed energy. Like a second wind, especially when he handed me a single red rose with a Christmas tree bow. It was so simple, yet so breathtakingly beautiful.

"What are you in the mood for?" he asks, glancing at the different options.

I already know my first choice, so I blurt out, "Pulled pork nachos."

Burk smiles widely. "I should have known. And a corn dog for dessert?"

A chuckle slides from my lips. "No corn dog this time, but that'll be on the menu for my next visit."

Nodding, he leads me toward the truck serving a variety of pulled pork and brisket options. The line is the longest here, so we settle in and prepare for the wait. But I don't mind. The food here is delicious, and the family who cooks and serves it a staple in our small community.

"Talked to Gramps earlier today," Burk says.

"Yeah?"

He nods and smiles. "He's really progressing through PT. Gram and he are having a movie night at the nursing home, and Uncle Karl and Aunt Sheila are going to visit him for a bit in the morning."

I open my mouth to ask a question but close it just as quickly. I'm not sure I should inquire, especially since it might be a rocky conversation, one I'm not part of.

"What?"

"Never mind, it's nothing," I backpedal.

"It's okay, Joy. You can ask."

I glance up and meet gentle brown eyes. Clearing my throat, I ask, "Have you talked to your parents? You know … about… everything?"

He nods. "I have. Dad was a little pissed they called me for help, but when I explained I had been communicating with Klint a bit, he backed off. Before I left, I sat down with him and said this was something I had to do. The fight was between them, and I wasn't taking sides. The family business needed help, and I was in a place to do it. He actually texted me a couple days ago and asked how Gramps was doing."

"That's good," I reply as we take a couple steps forward.

"It is. I don't know if they'll ever repair the damage to their relationship, but honestly, that's not my worry. I'm going to focus on mine and make sure things are square between me, my grandparents, and the rest of my extended family. I've lost so much time with them, and being back here now is a reminder of that. I told Gramps earlier I'd be willing to come back and help during the Christmas season. I might not be able to stay a month, but I can give the family business a solid two weeks, maybe more."

A wide grin takes over my face. "I'm sure he loved hearing that."

Burk returns the gesture and nods. "He did. Said I'm welcome anytime."

My heart starts to beat harder in my chest and the thought of not seeing Burk again for almost a year causes pain to erupt. In just a short amount of time, we've fallen back into old ways, and frankly, the thought of him returning to the other side of the country gives me palpitations.

I guess I'm just going to have to enjoy what I can while he's here.

"Hey, Joy!"

I look up and offer a warm greeting to Jennie Lancaster, the oldest of the three Lancaster daughters, all of whom help their parents at catering events and festivals. "Hi, Jennie. Looks to be another busy night," I tell her as she prepares to take our orders.

"It is. We're almost out of brisket," she informs us.

"Good to know," Burk replies, looking down at me. "Go ahead."

"I'll have the pulled pork nachos with sour cream and sweet pickles," I state, my stomach growling in anticipation.

"I'll have the brisket sandwich and fries, please," Burk orders.

"Drinks?" Jennie asks as she moves to their small cash register.

Burk lifts an eyebrow in question, and I reply, "I'm good. I think I'll have a cocoa from the church stand."

"They're so good," Jennie announces as she presses the buttons to total our bill. "They have that marshmallow syrup you can add. Almost tastes like a s'more."

"Oh, I'm definitely getting that," I say as Burk pulls out his wallet and hands over the money for our dinner. He even slips some in the tip jar on the counter.

To me, he hands me another twenty. "How about you go grab us a couple of cocoas, and we can meet at the pavilion. Looks like there's some tables left."

I nod but refuse to take the money. "Sounds good."

"Easy-Bake?" he hollers before I am able to take two steps away from him.

I glance over my shoulder and smirk when he holds up the twenty. "I got it, Burkey Turkey."

Making my way to where the cocoa stand is, I jump in line with the rest of the patrons ready for their cocoa fix. "Well, well, well, if it isn't my best friend."

I spin around and smile at Krista. "I thought you said you weren't coming," I remind her. At least that's what she said when she helped me at the bakery last night selling Christmas tree cakes and snowflake cookies.

She shrugs and glances around. "Well, who am I to miss an opportunity to find Mr. Right while eating a corn dog and riding the Tilt-A-Whirl."

I snort and take in the beautiful soft glow of the twinkle lights adorning every tree in the park. It hasn't snowed in a few days, but there's still a blanket of the white stuff covering the ground. It looks magical and pure. "I'll be rooting for you," I tell her.

Krista sighs. "How's the date going?"

"Good," I state, already grinning.

"You're so smitten," she mutters.

"Smitten?" I ask with a chuckle.

"Totally," she insists with a shrug. "You two are the cutest."

I take a step forward in the line and turn back to my friend. "It can't last though." Vocalizing what's been on my mind is hard, but it needs said.

Krista lifts her shoulders. "At least you know going into it though, right? I mean, he's only here until the end of the month. So...have fun. Have *fun*, if you know what I mean."

I feel heat burn my cheeks, because, yes, I know exactly what kind of fun she's referring to. "Won't that make it worse?"

"I suppose it could, but if your eyes are wide open going into it, you can protect your heart."

I just look at my friend, not sure I believe her. I can already feel my heart getting way more invested than it should, but I think I can chalk a big part of that up to the familiarity Burk invokes. He was my closest friend for so long for a reason. We just click.

"I guess," I reply, not sounding the least bit convinced.

"All I'm saying is enjoy it. You deserve this. Especially after numbnuts treated you terribly. You need some happy. Some good sex, and something tells me that man can deliver."

I glance to my left, following her line of sight, and practically choke on the crisp air. "How do you know?" I whisper, watching as he takes our food toward the pavilion to secure a table.

"It's written all over his face and body language. Do you know he's looked over here no less than six times in the last three minutes?"

Instantly, I smile. "Yeah?"

"Uhh huh," she replies. "Now, step forward and order your drinks before he abandons your food and comes over here to find out what's taking so long."

I look back at the line and realize I'm next to order. "Hi, sorry, Janelle," I tell the woman manning the money box at the cocoa stand. "Can I get two hot cocoas with marshmallow syrup, please?"

"Of course," she replies, relaying the order to the high schoolers making the beverages.

"Five dollars."

I hand over the cash and slip a few extra bills into the tip jar. It all goes back to the church and helps fund their annual Christmas pageant. "I heard your sister and the Mitchell boy are getting married," Janelle says, a sad look crossing her face.

"Uhh, yeah. They're planning a small ceremony for Christmas."

Janelle sighs. "Sadie is so heartbroken."

"Sadie? Your daughter?" I ask, trying to piece it all together but coming up short.

"Yes, Sadie. She's always had a thing for John. I thought they might end up together," she tells me wistfully.

"Oh, uhhh..."

"Awkward," Krista mutters behind me.

"Here you go, Joy," the girl announces as she sets my hot cocoas on the small table.

"Thank you, Bella." Picking up the drinks, I say to Janelle, "Have a good evening."

She sort of mumbles a reply and lifts her nose, but I ignore her. To Krista, I reply, "If you want, you're welcome to come ice skating with us."

My friend makes a horrified face. "And be a third wheel? No thank you."

I bark out a laugh and shake my head. "Offer stands."

With that, I head to the pavilion to where Burk waits. As I approach the picnic table where he's sitting, he stands up and gives me a smile. "Everything all right?"

"Yes, Krista was behind me in line," I inform him, setting the insulated cups down on the table and taking a seat. "I hope you're extra hungry, because there's no way I'll eat all of this."

He chuckles. "I admit, when she set it on the counter, I was shocked by the quantity of food."

I reach for my first chip coated in pulled pork, cheddar cheese, and sweet BBQ sauce. "It's way too much food for one person, but it's my favorite. I should have told you we could share." After I chew, I use another chip to scoop the toppings up and hand it across the table.

"Thanks," he says, taking a big bite. "Wow, that's good," he adds after chewing. "Want some?"

I know he's offering me some of his food, but that's not where my brain goes. Suddenly, I'm a fifteen-year-old boy and thinking about sex.

Again.

"No thank you," I respond as we dive into our delicious food. We chat about everything, from work that day to family and friends. We catch up on town gossip, and I do my best to fill him in on what's happened with classmates we had over the years. It's comfortable, and every time someone stops by to say hello, Burk is gracious and friendly.

When our meals have been consumed—or at least most of mine—he jumps up and throws our containers in the trash. "Are you ready?"

"For ice skating? I'm always ready," I declare with a big smile.

"Do we need to run back to your place to get your skates?" he asks.

Even though my apartment is literally across the square, I shake my head. "I'm just going to use theirs. It'll be easier and quicker."

"We can run back. It won't take long."

I appreciate the offer, but it's not necessary. On the weekends, during festival hours, you can rent skates. "No, really. I usually just rent them on nights like tonight." I use my own during the times the rink is available but the skates aren't.

"All right," he announces with the clap of his hands. "Let's do this."

"I'm going to feel this tomorrow," Burk announces between fits of laughter. He's sprawled out on the ice, having fallen for the second time.

A giggle slips from my lips, and I try to cover it with my gloved hand. "You need a little practice is all."

He starts to stand up, and I reach out to help keep him steady. "My ego is taking a huge hit tonight," he grumbles good-heartedly.

"I'm sure your ego is plenty padded," I tease as he returns to his full height.

His eyebrows pull up in question. "Is that an ass joke?"

I can't stop the laughter once more. "You're nuts."

"Because my ass might have some extra padding, but I've been told it's one of my finest features," he quips, reminding me of one of our early conversations where I basically told him his ass was nice.

Grinning, I take his hand, and we start to skate once more. We make several laps around the rink, and a huge wave of contentment washes over me.

"You okay?"

"Yeah, why?" I ask, turning my attention his way.

"You sighed."

"Oh," I reply, feeling heat warm my cheeks. "I'm just...happy. This is my favorite time of year, and we're doing one of my favorite activities. It's such a beautiful night with the twinkle lights surrounding us and the holiday music. It feels magical, and I'm just...yeah." My blush deepens. "Plus, the company isn't so bad either."

He glances down and grins widely. "The company may be my favorite part."

We skate around the rink for a while, talking and just enjoying our time together. I know this isn't one of his favorite activities, but he never complains. Just holds my hand and skates beside me as we circle the ice.

Two young kids zoom past us, laughing and carrying on as the boy hollers, "Too slow!"

"Punks," Burk mutters, making me laugh.

"That's the exact same thing we used to do at that age," I remind him as the young boy and girl spin circles around some of the other skaters.

"Yeah, but that boy has talent. I did not," he grumbles as the boy starts to move backward with ease and confidence.

I giggle and shake my head. "You're doing just fine."

"Yeah, well my best asset is going to be bruised tomorrow morning," he mumbles, cracking the hint of a smile.

Just then, the two younger kids come by once more. This time, the young boy spins a circle in front of Burk, and what happens next can only be described as chaos. Burk tries to stop so he doesn't run into the boy but ends of shifting to the side. Unfortunately, when he does that, his body pitches somewhat violently and his feet start to dance.

Not in the good way either.

In the flash of a second, he realizes he's going down, so his grip on me tightens as he attempts to stabilize himself.

It doesn't work.

The next thing I know, we're both crashing to the cold, frozen rink in a pile of limbs and pain. My head is kept from hitting the unforgiving surface by being rolled. Before my brain can catch up with what's happening, I'm lying on top of Burk, his gorgeous face registering pain.

"Shit," he mutters. "I'm so sorry, are you all right?"

"I'm fine," I insist, trying not to dwell on the fact my body is pressed against his and feels fucking amazing.

"Did you hit your head?" he asks, searching my face with worry.

"No, I'm fine. You?"

He shifts a little and his face scrunches up in discomfort. "I think I dislocated my ass."

I bark out a laugh, my focus quickly returning to the fact my breasts shift and rub his chest as I giggle. When our eyes connect, his seem to sober instantly, as if he's suddenly realizing we're pressed together very intimately. Not to mention the fact one of his hands is resting on my ass.

Clearing his throat, he suddenly moves. But it's not either of his hands, it's his mouth. He plasters his lips to mine, his tongue delving deep as he tastes. I feel my body explode like a firecracker. It's instant, intense, and burns me in the best way possible.

"I'm sorry!"

Burk and I startle, our kiss—and the moment—broken. We both turn to see the young boy who caused us to stumble and fall crouching beside where we lie. "It's okay, buddy. I'm not nearly as good of a skater as you are," Burk tells the young boy, who offers a wide grin.

"I practice a lot. But my mom says I shouldn't be so cocky and give the other people space," he informs us, as if Mom had a hand in his apology.

"It's all good, buddy. Thank you for apologizing," Burk replies, carefully rolling me off his body and helping me sit up.

"You should practice your swizzles and crossovers."

I giggle but quickly cover it with a cough and a hand to my mouth.

Burk, clearly realizing my laughter comes at his expense, narrows his eyes at me before turning a smile at the boy. "You're right, I should get some more practice in."

"Okay! Bye!" the boy declares before taking off like a bolt of lightning and heading to where the young girl waits for him.

"Well, I do believe I was just told by a seven-year-old."

Another giggle slips from my mouth. I seem to be doing a lot of that when I'm around Burk. "How's your ass-et?" I ask, the innuendo hanging heavy between us.

"Sore," he informs me. Carefully, he stands up before reaching both hands down to me. "Shall we?"

Placing my hands in his, I get up from the ice and stand directly in front of him. The tension grows thick once more, crackling like logs in a fireplace. The heat coming from his body and his eyes mirrors that of my own, and all I want to do is get back to my place and be alone with this man.

The one who started off as a friend, until the lines started to blur.

And that's exactly what has happened since he arrived back in town.

I want more.

From Burk.

There's no turning back.

Chapter Fourteen

Burk

The feel of her body splayed along mine will forever be branded in my head. As I take her hand and practically drag her off the rink, I have to tell myself to slow it down. There's no reason for me to maul her right here in the middle of the festival, with Santa, Mrs. Claus, and the rest of the busybodies to witness.

The moment we're out of the rink, we head for one of the benches where we left our shoes. Joy takes a seat and starts removing her skates, with me hot on her heels. There's an urgency hanging heavily in the air, a sexual tension that's driving us both.

"I'm so sorry about Jonah," a woman says, stopping in front of where we're sitting. "He gets a little carried away on the ice."

"It's okay," Joy tells her, offering a friendly smile.

"He's been taking skating lessons, and he sometimes forgets he's out there for fun and not playing hockey," she replies with a chuckle.

"He's a great skater," I say, finishing taking off my first skate and shoving my foot into my boot.

"Are either of you hurt?"

"No," Joy replies at the same time I say, "Only my ego, since I was shown up by a kid."

The woman seems to relax, offering us both a smile. "Well, I'm glad. And I'm happy neither of you were hurt."

The moment I have my second skate off and boot on, I stand up and meet her grin with my own. "We're fine, but thank you for checking. Merry Christmas."

"Merry Christmas to you both," she replies before returning to the edge of the rink where she was watching her kids skate.

"That was nice of her," Joy says, standing up and reaching for her skates.

"It was," I agree, taking her empty hand and practically dragging her toward the rental stand.

We return the skates to the table, and I quickly slip a tip into the jar before wrapping my hand around hers and dragging her away. Not literally, but there's definitely a hurry to my gait. It's like each step I take gets me closer to her apartment.

Just as we reach the sidewalk on the opposite side of the rink, I stop and face her. "I'm sorry, I'm not meaning to rush. Is there anything else you wanted to see or do?"

She slowly shakes her head, meeting my gaze. "Nope. I'm fine with heading back to my place."

Nodding, I watch for a break in traffic, which consists of one car passing by, and carefully navigate us past the parked cars and toward the alley behind her building. Joy unlocks the door, and we slip inside, heading up the stairs to her place.

Once we're in the warm space, she starts to strip out of her boots, gloves, hat, and coat. Her hair is a little mussed, but all I can think about is how it would look in the morning, splayed across her pillow. Joy wears very little makeup, and I envision it smudged beneath her eyes as she rouses from a deep sleep.

"What?" she asks with a touch of hesitation.

"I love your hair," I reply, recognizing the change she's made. "You're beautiful."

A rosy blush covers her cheeks as she gives me a shy little grin. "I don't know about that."

"I do. The most beautiful woman in my world."

I reach and pull her into my arms. When my hands wrap around her waist, it's then I realize I haven't removed my winter wear. I quickly rip my gloves off my hands and drop them where I stand. My stocking cap goes next, followed by my thick coat. When I step out of my boots, I finally pull her toward me once more. This time, there's only a regular clothing barrier between us, one I hope to discard soon.

If she says yes, of course.

"Is it okay if I kiss you again?"

"I'd be incredibly disappointed if you didn't," she whispers, eliminating any space between us.

When my lips brush hers, it's as if I'm zapped with faulty Christmas lights. A zing of electricity jolts through my veins, causing the most breathtaking mixture of pleasure and pain. It devours me like a raging fire, burning me in the best way.

The only way.

I let the flames consume me willingly.

As if engaged in an orchestrated dance, we move backward until her ass bumps the counter. When she hitches her right leg up, her heel circling to the back of my thigh, I step to her body and revel in the feel of her softness against my hardness. Joy mewls, rocking her hips against my erection. The friction is glorious, better than a tree full of presents on Christmas morning.

I want more.

Reaching behind her, I gently lift her up and deposit her onto the countertop. From this position, she's able to wrap both legs around my waist, bringing the heat of her pussy in direct contact with my cock. It surges with need, thickening even more as desire grabs hold.

Any doubt I might have had about her wanting this as much as I do evaporates like water in the desert the moment she reaches between us and slides her hand long the length of me. I groan, unable to stop the sound. "Hell, Joy," I mutter, closing my eyes as the pleasure courses through me.

"Nope, I'm going for Heaven, Burk," she murmurs, cupping me firmly.

Friction.

So much glorious friction.

"I needed to get your attention, in case you were entertaining thoughts of slowing this down or that I'm not one-hundred-percent on board with this."

"You have my undivided attention," I grumble, my heart trying to beat out of my chest. I have to close my eyes to try to ward off the pleasure she's evoking, but really it doesn't help. If anything, it makes it worse because I'm left alone with just my thoughts, and those are really, *really* fucking dirty.

"Good, because I know the man you are, and you're probably worrying about crossing lines and morning regrets. Well, I'm here to reassure you there will be none of either. I want this, Burk. I want this with *you*."

Opening my eyes, I watch the storm brewing in the depths of her green eyes. It's a heady mixture of lust and raw need, and a burst of pride swells in my chest when I see it. I did that. I put that look in her eyes, on her face. All I want to do now is prove to her I'm the only man to finish the job.

Sliding my hands up the column of her neck, my fingertips slip into her hair as I angle her head and claim her lips once more. She tastes like heaven, her body molding to mine like a second skin. Joy opens her mouth, granting my tongue access to take and plunder. The kiss transforms into something dirtier quickly as hands start to move, gripping at clothes and tugging them off.

My Henley is pushed up, her fingers dancing across my fevered skin. We break the kiss long enough for me to help pull it over my head and toss it onto the floor. Her sweater goes next, exposing first the soft skin of her stomach and then the glorious mounds of her breasts.

Joy lifts her arms, granting me permission to remove her sweater completely. It joins mine on the floor somewhere behind me. I take her jaw in my hands and press my lips to hers once more. Our tongues dance together as she wraps her arms around me, pulling her chest flush against mine. Her breasts flatten against my skin, the thin, silky bra doing nothing to conceal the hardness of her nipples.

Ripping my mouth from hers, I trail it across her jaw and down her neck. I get a better view of her bra, smiling when I see the small ice-skating bears dancing across the material. I chuckle, swiping my thumb across first one hard nipple, then the second. "Jesus, you're so beautiful."

Joy gasps when I lean forward and draw one nipple between my lips. Even through the material, I can feel it tighten more, making my mouth water. I glance up and watch her eyes as I gently pull the left cup of her bra down like I'm revealing a Christmas surprise. And maybe that's exactly what I am doing.

My prize.

Swirling my tongue over the exposed nipple, I feel her entire body tighten as her back arches. She reaches for me, her fingers diving into my hair as she pulls me closer. I draw the tight bud into my mouth and suck greedily, practically getting off on the moan erupting from her mouth.

That's when an idea hits me.

As much as I want to devour her in the kitchen, the thought of seeing her splayed out in another way takes root in my brain. Slipping my hands beneath her ass and moving my mouth to hers, I lift her off the counter and spin toward the living room. Her arms wrap around my neck, her body molded to my chest, as I devour her with a kiss. When we reach the living room, I move to the couch and deposit her onto the cushions. "Don't move."

Moving fast, I plug in the lights on her Christmas tree, which she only leaves on if she's home, and then start grabbing from the pile of blankets she keeps in a large basket beside the couch. Once I have a nice, thick "bed" made beside the tree, I turn my attention back to the woman who completely captivates me.

Extending my hand, she takes it immediately and stands up. My eyes feast on her beauty, from her mussed hair to her exposed nipple, down to her long legs, even though they're still covered.

My fingers glide across her stomach as they make their way to the fly of her jeans. When her muscles tighten, I can't help but smile. "Still ticklish, I see."

Her eyes narrow just a bit. "Be nice, Burkey Turkey."

"Oh, don't you worry your pretty little head, Easy-Bake. I'm about to be very *nice.*"

Her grin holds a hint of naughty as she bites down on her bottom lip. With our eyes locked, she reaches down and releases the button on her jeans and lowers the zipper, as if she can't wait another second for me to do it. That's okay though. Even if I'd much rather prefer to strip her naked myself, I can't deny the view of her taking off her pants is something that'll stay with me for the rest of my life.

She pushes both her jeans and the winter insulated long johns she had on beneath them down her legs, carefully stepping out of them and kicking them to the side. "Now you."

With the flash of a grin, I mirror the steps until I'm standing in just my boxer briefs. Reaching for my wallet, I pull out the condom I placed there the day before. Not that I was expecting to get to this point with Joy, but you never know. Better safe than sorry. If I were a Boy Scout, I'd get a badge for being prepared.

One eyebrow shoots upward in question, and all I do is shrug. "Not gonna lie and say I haven't been hoping to get to this point, Joy, but if it wasn't tonight, I would have been fine and still had one of the best dates I've ever had."

Reaching up, she strokes my scruffy jaw and flashes a small, yet impactful grin. "Same."

Going up on her tiptoes, she closes the space between us and kisses me. The moment our mouths meet, time just seems to stop. That may sound weird to say, but it's the only way to describe it. The world completely fades away, and we're the only two people left.

Carefully, I help her lie on the makeshift bed I created with blankets and smile. She glows like the lights on the tree, and when I see them reflecting off her radiant skin and hypnotic green eyes, I can't help but feel like I'm the luckiest son of a bitch on the planet right now.

Tonight, she's mine.

Covering her body with my own, her legs wrap around my waist, drawing us back together. I take her lips, gently at first but then more insistent as she rocks her hips against me. The barrier of our underwear prevents me from thrusting deep inside her body the way I crave, but that's okay. It keeps me present and reminds me to savor this moment.

Ripping my mouth from hers, I give her a cocky little grin and say, "Be right back."

Then, I move.

Slowly, I climb down her body, stopping at her breasts. Reaching behind her back, I'm able to unclasp her bra and expose both glorious tits. Holding one in my hand, I draw the tight little bud between my lips and nip at the flesh.

"Oh God," she mutters with a gasp.

I swirl my tongue around the bud, gently drawing it between my lips and deep into my mouth. Her hands dive into my hair as she starts writhing beneath me. When I'm satisfied I've showered it with enough pleasure, I move to the other and do the same. Joy doesn't have huge tits, but there's enough of a handful for me to play with. Her nipples are a rosy red color, just like her cheeks are right now.

Now, I move farther down her body, licking her stomach and placing open-mouthed kisses against her flesh. Reaching the apex of her legs, I glance up and meet her gaze. "Yes?"

She nods insistently. "Hell yes."

Smiling, I pull off her panties with little skating bears on them and dive in. The first swipe of my tongue is electric. Her taste, her wetness coats me, driving me for more. Joy's legs spread, giving me access to what I crave, so I do exactly what a man with his face buried in the pussy of the woman he wants more than anything does.

I devour.

Sucking her clit into my mouth, Joy gasps and grinds against my face. I continue to lap at her core, alternating between licking and sucking before bringing my fingers into the mix. Sliding a single finger into her hot, wet pussy, I'm rewarded with the feel of her internal muscles quivering around me. She's close, and I'm going to push her over the edge.

Slipping a second finger inside, I revel in the tightness surrounding me and focus my attention on her clit. Her hips move, her body hums with need as I flatten my tongue against her clit and lick with pressure.

"So close," she whispers, gyrating and chasing her looming release.

As much as I'd love to draw this out, watching her come has quickly become a need of my own. With two fingers deep inside her, I latch on to her clit and gently lift my fingertips in a come-hither motion. The movement works perfectly, and I feel her entire body tighten as she detonates like a bomb.

Joy comes hard, her pussy squeezing my fingers and her entire body goes rigid and taut. She starts to shake as she cries out my name, and second to her taste, it's the sweetest thing ever. I want to hear it over and over as she comes, my name falling from her lips.

When her release subsides, I sit up and wipe the wetness coating my mouth. Her eyes are glazed over, her naked body sated, and I've never seen her more breathtaking. Crawling back up her body,

I press my lips against hers. If she's turned off by her taste on my tongue she doesn't let on. In fact, she wraps her arms around my neck and deepens the kiss.

"I'm not done with you," I murmur against her lips before trailing mine down her neck.

"Thank God," she replies, shivering beneath my touch.

Moving to my knees, I grab the condom I had retrieved and rip open the package. I quickly stand, pushing my underwear down my legs. My erection bounces free, hard and ready for what's to come. I quickly cover myself in protection and return to the floor where Joy waits.

Coming down on top of her once more, she wraps her arms and legs tightly around me. My cock is pinned between our bodies, desperate to feel her tightness engulf me. But before I do, there's something I need to say.

"Joy," I start, holding her gaze as I set my elbows on either side of her head.

She reaches up and strokes my jaw. "I know, Burk."

Still needing to say the words, I continue, "I'm only here until the end of the month."

She gives me a smile full of sadness. "I know. I *know* that. And I don't care. I'll take you any way I can get you, for as long as you're here."

Relief washes over me. Not at the thought of leaving her in a very short couple of weeks, but the fact she understands. She knows the sand in the hourglass is slowly trickling away, and yet she still wants to be with me. It's a heady feeling, one I don't take lightly.

I brush my lips across hers and murmur, "Then we make the most of my time until our time runs out." I kiss across her jaw and behind her ear.

She shivers, arching her back up and pressing her chest against mine. "I can live with that."

And with that, I adjust my position and slowly press inside her pussy.

When I'm completely seated inside her, that's when it hits me.

She might be able to live with it, but I'm not sure I can.

Chapter Fifteen

Joy

My body ignites as he pushes inside me. It's a tight fit, but the moment he takes my lips with his, I feel myself starting to relax. Then, he moves, and any thought of relaxation flies right out the window.

Burk rocks his hips, gently pushing forward before pulling himself almost completely out. Just as I start to show my displeasure with him, he thrusts. I cry out as pleasure consumes me. It doesn't matter I already had one orgasm, I can feel a second one brewing. I crave it.

I crave him.

Hitching my legs higher on his hips, I open them wider and draw him deeper. A moan pulls from my lungs, stealing my breath. He grinds his pubis against my clit causing a second orgasm to start to build. His pace starts to pick up as he fills me hard and fast. Burk moves his mouth to my ear, sucking my earlobe into his mouth before whispering, "I want to feel you come, Joy."

I whimper, digging my nails into the flesh of his back as my release begins. It's like a tsunami pulling back from the coast, growing bigger and building pressure until it finally lets go, destroying everything in its path. I come hard, crying out Burk's name as wave after wave of pleasure washes over me.

"Fuck," he groans just before he goes completely still. He closes his eyes and starts to pump, slow at first, but then faster as he empties himself inside me. When neither of us have anything left, he falls on top of me, caging me to the floor with his arms and legs.

I wrap my arms around his neck and take a deep breath. "Wow."

He grunts a reply and drops his forehead to rest against mine. "Watching you come on my mouth was spectacular, but seeing and feeling it on my cock is a whole different level of amazing."

"Mmmm," I murmur, closing my eyes and just breathing him in.

Burk swipes his lips gently across my lips and whispers, "Stay here. I need to take care of the condom."

He carefully gets up and slips away, leaving me sated and smiling on my living room floor. I look over at the Christmas tree, the lights twinkling brightly, and realize this was the perfect spot for our first time. We decorated this tree together, and then we got naked and busy beneath it.

I can't help but giggle a little.

"What's so funny?" he asks, returning to where he left me.

The laughter on my lips dies as I stare up at his very naked, very beautiful body. I'm not sure I've ever considered a man beautiful before, but really there's no other way to describe him. He's toned in all the right places, his long, strong legs powerful as he walks. And let's not forget what's hanging between his legs. Even soft, he's every woman's fantasy.

"Joy?" he asks, amusement dancing in his eyes.

"I was just thinking about how we decorated this tree and then had sex under it."

A cocky grin transforms his entire face. "We did." Handing over a warm washcloth, he says, "Here."

I take it, even though I'll need to get up and use the bathroom soon. But all thoughts of getting up evaporate from my mind when he grabs another thick blanket and climbs onto the makeshift bed with me. Setting the cloth aside, I curl into his embrace, letting the warmth of his body cocoon me.

A sigh spills from my lips as I rest my cheek against his chest, and he pulls the blanket over us. "This is nice," I murmur, my eyes closing.

"I agree," he replies, placing a kiss on my forehead.

"Sleep, Easy-Bake."

I nod, my body being lulled to sleep by the steady beat of his heart and the heaviness of my limbs and achiness between my legs.

Using the bathroom can wait a bit.

Falling asleep in Burk's arms is the only thing on my mind as I drift off to sleep.

I'm stirred from the most glorious sleep by lips softly pressing against my neck. They trail lightly up to that magically sensitive spot behind my ear. "Good morning," he murmurs, his warm breath tickling my flesh.

"Hi," I practically mewl, gently stretching my legs.

"It's still early, but I'm gonna need to get up soon and head out."

Something hits me, and before I can vocalize my question, I feel my face heat up. "Umm, did you, huh, tell anyone you were here?"

He flashes a quick grin and nods. "I texted Gram last night after you fell asleep to let her know I was staying with a friend."

The blush I feel grows even hotter. "Did you tell her..."

"No, but I'm pretty sure she knows who my friend is. She seemed very happy when she replied. Used several heart emojis."

I cover my eyes with my hand and groan. "Oh, man."

He reaches for my hand and pulls it away from my face. There's a hint of worry in his eyes as he asks, "Do you not want anyone to know I'm here?"

"What? No," I quickly refute realizing he took my statement the wrong way. "I don't care who knows you spent the night, Burk. Honestly. I just know how this town works, and they'll probably have us married by the end of the day."

He snorts, running his hand up my side. "Seems a little fast, even by Snowflake Falls standards."

My body is humming as his hand makes its way to my breast. "You seem to have forgotten just how fast gossip travels here."

Burk rolls over, sliding his body between my open legs. "Know what else moves fast?" He presses his lips against mine in a firm, chaste kiss. "Me."

He spends the next thirty minutes showing me exactly how fast he moves.

I step inside the small dressing room at the boutique, and just before I can lock the door behind me, it bursts open. "You had sex!" my sister whisper-yells.

"What?" I ask, gaping guiltily at her.

"I knew it! I can tell." She grins victoriously at me, the smugness ebbing off her in waves.

With my hands on my hips, I forget all about the dark-red velvet dress hanging on the hook. "How?"

"You're glowing," she confirms, walking over to the dress and running her hand over the crushed velvet material. When she turns back to face me, she adds, "You look happy."

I glance away, afraid she'll see exactly how happy I truly am. He makes me want—and feel—things I shouldn't. Especially for a girl who knows how this ends. He leaves. I stay. End of story.

"You're falling for him," she murmurs gently.

Returning my gaze to hers, I nod. "I shouldn't."

"Why not?" she asks, taking a seat in the chair beside the door.

"Because he's not staying here, Eve. He's…temporary."

She stands up and goes to the dress, removing it from the hanger and making an up-and-down motion with her hand. I know that's code for me to strip. I do as instructed and get down to the strapless bra and panties I wore for today's dress search. "But you knew that before you slept with him."

Taking the dress, I carefully step into it and pull it up my frame. "I know."

My sister moves to my back and starts to zip the dress, not saying a word until the beautiful dress is in place and she gazes at me through the mirror. "Maybe he won't go."

I scoff at her comment, wishing she wouldn't have spoken my truest wish aloud. Why? Because I know it won't happen. He's told me as much from the beginning, but that doesn't stop my heart from wanting what it wants.

"I know," she replies softly, stepping forward and hugging me from behind. Her smile is sad as she gazes at me through the mirror. "I'm sorry."

I exhale slowly, waves of my own sadness washing over me. "Don't be. It's not anyone's fault."

"But still. I'm sorry this hurts you."

Turning around, I stare at my older sister, the one who finally found true love. "I know what I'm doing is going to hurt, Eve. And even though I'm well aware of how this is going to turn out for me, I still want to cross the line. Because the thought of not spending what little time I get with him somehow feels worse than the alternative. Does that make sense?" I ask, desperate for someone to understand me.

She nods. "Yeah, it does. You'd rather be with him for those few weeks, knowing it'll end with your heart broken, than break it off now and miss that time."

Though she gets it, it still doesn't make it any easier. I feel tears well in my eyes, and I try to blink them away. "How did this happen? How did I fall for him so fast?"

Her eyes are sad as she grins at me. "You've probably always loved him, Joy. Maybe not in the exact way, but you two were inseparable growing up. The kind of love built from solid friendship. Even though you guys were young doesn't mean it wasn't there. So it would be logical that love would grow into something bigger later in life."

I nod. "Yeah." Her statement feels right. "I just..." I swallow over the lump in my throat. "I'm going to hate it when he leaves."

I'm pulled into a fierce hug. "I know, Joy."

I give myself several seconds to soak up the comfort and love my sister is giving me, and when I pull back, I sniffle and offer a smile. "Thanks."

"I'm always here for you, little sister."

"And I'm always here for you," I confirm. "Now, enough of my drama." Turning to finally take in my reflection in the mirror, I gasp, "Wow."

She steps into view and is grinning from ear to ear. "You look amazing."

The deep-red, floor-length dress hugs my figure in the best way. It has a slit up the left leg, is off the shoulder, and has three-quarter length sleeves. Plus, a subtle V at my chest that gives a hint of cleavage without giving away the farm, if you know what I mean. It's the perfect color and style for a winter Christmas wedding. "This is so pretty," I whisper, taking in the beautiful dress.

"It's perfect," she assures me. "And it doesn't even look like you need alterations."

I continue to scrutinize my appearance in the mirror, and even though I'm sure she's a bit biased, I do admit this gown is pretty dang close to perfection. "You think this is the one?" I ask, my heart starting to pound in my chest.

"Are you kidding me? If you tried on another dress, I'd be pissed at you. This one was made for you."

I nod, taking in my reflection one more time.

"Burk is going to swallow his tongue when he sees you," she declares, offering a wink. "I can't wait."

I bark out a laugh and shake my head. "Okay, I choose this one. Let me get out of it, and we can find you a dress," I say, turning my back to my sister so she can unzip me.

When we arrived, Eve insisted on finding my maid of honor dress first, as well as giving the moms time to find theirs. She said part of the joy in this experience was watching us choose our dresses too, and she wanted to be completely present for that part. "I'm going to step out and see if the others have found any to try on," she says, referring to our mom, John's Mom, Patti, and his grandma, Glenda.

I nod and wait until the door is closed behind her. When I'm left alone, I take a deep, calming breath. I probably shouldn't have burdened this day with the heaviness hanging on my heart, but I knew my sister would understand. And like any other time we've talked, she helped me work through what was troubling me.

The fact remains that I'm falling hard and fast for Burk, and even though he's leaving, I'm still going to see this through. My heart might be completely shattered by the time New Year's Eve rolls around, but the thought of not sharing these last couple of weeks with him feels almost more soul-crushing. I know how this will end. I'm choosing to enjoy the ride until that time comes.

When my dress is on the hanger and my clothes are back on, I step out into the small dressing room area and smile. Both my mom and John's are standing in the middle of the row of mirrors wearing beautiful dresses. Both have chosen a shade a green and look equally beautiful.

"What do you think?" Mom asks me.

"You both look stunning," I assure her.

Glenda is sitting in a wingback chair, smiling widely. "I agree. They look exquisite."

Mom makes a face. "You aren't going to show me the dress?"

I give her an apologetic look and hand the dress to the sales associate. "Sorry, I didn't think to come out and show everyone."

"I think it's the perfect dress," Eve states before turning to Glenda. "Have you found a dress?"

The older woman waves her hand. "I'm just along for the ride, dear. I have plenty of dresses in my closet I can wear."

"John insisted," Eve replies to the older woman.

"How many times is your only grandson going to get married?" Patti asks.

"Well, he better only get married once," my sister replies with a hint of sarcasm.

"Oh, I have no doubt about it," Glenda vows, slowly standing from her seat and taking the few steps to where Eve stands. She takes her hand and adds, "I've never seen my grandson so in love. You've made him happier than I could have ever wanted, and I have no doubt in my mind and my heart that this love will last forever."

My sister sniffles and smiles. "Thanks, Grandma Glenda."

"You're welcome, dear. Now, I know my grandson insisted I get a new dress too, but really, it's not necessary. I have so many clothes that I never wear, and I know I have something perfect already hanging in my closet. In fact, I have something in mind."

"You do?" Eve asks, wiping a few stray tears from her cheeks.

"I do," Glenda assures. "I've even already tried it on."

"Well, if you're sure. John said he'd be happy to buy you a new dress, since everyone else is getting something new."

Glenda smiles lovingly at my sister and squeezes her hand. "My grandson has a heart of gold, but I do not need him to buy me a new dress. The one I'm wearing was actually a gift from his grandfather. He purchased it for me right before he passed away, and sadly, I never got to wear it. I see no better occasion to bring it out of the back of the closet than our only grandson's wedding. So, please tell John I appreciate his offer, but I'm going to decline."

My sister bursts into tears and throws her arms around the older woman's shoulders. Glenda returns the gesture, holding her future granddaughter-in-law tightly. "I can't wait to see it."

She grins and pats my sister's hand. "You know what I can't wait to see? You in the dress you're going to marry my grandson in. We're all situated, so now it's your turn, dear. Let's find you a wedding dress."

My sister beams brighter than the North Star shining in the sky. "I can't wait."

"Go," Glenda urges.

Eve takes my hand and leads me out to a section for off-the-rack bridal gowns. There are dresses of every shape and style, but she bypasses the ones I thought she'd gravitate toward and moves to one I wasn't expecting. "I want to try this one on," she tells the sales associate who followed us.

I gasp, my eyes wide as I watch the clerk remove the dress from the display mannequin.

"As soon as we stepped inside and I saw it, I knew," my sister tells me, her green eyes full of unshed tears.

"Yes," I agree, my heart beating wildly in my chest as we head toward the dressing room.

I'm prepared to stay outside and let Eve and the sales associate do their thing, but she latches on to my hand and pulls me inside. "I want your help."

Together, the clerk and I assist my sister into the formfitting, lace dress in a soft ivory. There's a short train with beautiful floral lace detail and ivory pearl buttons that go from the base of the spine all the way up to the neck. The front is even more stunning with a plunging neckline, but is covered with the lace, and sleeves that show off the intricate detail of the delicate material.

"What do you think?"

I meet her gaze, not even sure when I started to cry. "You look...so beautiful."

"Yeah?" my sister asks, turning her attention to her reflection. "I love it," she whispers, more to herself than to the clerk and me, but I couldn't agree more.

"It's your dress."

She turns, running her hands down the dress. "Shall we go show the others?"

I nod, moving to the door and pulling it open. I find three women anxiously sitting in the chairs, waiting to see the bride-to-be. "Are you ready?" I ask, earning a resounding yes from all three.

My sister walks out and all you hear are gasps. No one says a word as she walks to the round, elevated platform and steps up on top.

"Holy shit. My grandson is going to swallow his tongue."

We all laugh at Glenda's comment, yet no one disagrees.

"What do you think?" She looks at our mom first, who's openly crying.

Mom nods, wiping tears from her face as she replies, "I've never seen a more beautiful bride."

That's all it takes. There's not a dry eye in the building, including the sales associate who's standing off to the side, ready to help. She retrieves a box of tissues from the table and hands them out before taking one for herself. "This dress was special, and the moment you walked in and eyed it, I knew you'd be the one to wear it. It was actually an oops when we placed our last order, but when we unwrapped it, it was just too pretty to send back. I suspected the perfect bride for it was out there, and then you put it on. It was destined to be yours."

And just like that, we're all crying again.

We stand there for a while, oohing and awwing over the most stunning wedding dress on the face of the planet. John's Grandma

Glenda agrees to do a few alterations so it's not quite so long, but for the most part, the clerk is right. This dress was made for Eve.

In less than two weeks, she'll wear it as she pledges her eternal love and devotion to the one man she plans to spend the rest of her life with. What a beautiful fairy tale for John and Eve, and I'm so honored to be part of it.

I only wish there were a happily ever after in my own future.

Not today.

Not necessarily tomorrow.

But somewhere in the future.

I can only hope my story is as poetic and forever as my sister's.

Chapter Sixteen

Burk

"How was your night?"

I turn around and narrow my eyes at my cousin. He's smiling widely, clearly having heard about my text to Gram, even though I returned to the farm well before it was time for work. "None of your business."

He barks out a laugh. "Keep telling yourself that," he replies. "Everything is everyone's business in Snowflake Falls. Surely you haven't been gone so long you've forgotten that."

I glance to the left, spotting Joy's dad heading our way, and keep my mouth shut.

"Hey, Burk. I gotta bring up another load of greenery. Can you help me?" Ray asks, his face unreadable.

"Sure," I tell him, walking away from Klint and heading toward the back of the barn. A nervous energy surrounds me. Even though it's nearing the end of the workday, we've been busy enough I haven't really been around Ray. He was already on the tractor and bringing up a few pre-cut trees when I got down to the barn, and I've been running between the barn and the tree farm, helping customers cut down trees all day long.

"Been busy today," he says as we approach the rear side door.

"Yep. Must have cut down two dozen trees today," I tell him, slipping inside and walking to the bench. We offer greenery bundles made from broken branches or those we cut from the bottoms of trees. A lot of people buy them for decorations, while some make things like grave blankets out of them.

"There's usually an uptick of sales about two weeks out. Most likely, we've seen the biggest spike in sales now. We'll still sell trees right up to Christmas, but this weekend was probably our big one," he tells me, having already bundled and wrapped the greenery for easy sale.

"Well, I wouldn't mind a bit of a slowdown. I'm not used to so much manual labor," I reply with a chuckle.

Ray turns his attention my way. "You're doing great, Burk. And stop selling yourself short. Something tells me that job of yours can be pretty labor intensive too."

I swallow and think about building furniture. "Yeah, it is. It's just not as consistent with moving heavy material as this is."

He waves his hand. "Potato, po-tah-toe. Both hardworking, labor-intensive jobs, doing things with your hands and brain." When he makes no move to grab a stack of the greenery, I wait him out. "Cindy and I were looking at your social media pages last night."

A lump forms in my throat, and even though I want to grab my phone and see what it is they could have possibly seen, I stand here and keep my eyes locked on his.

"You're very good, Burk."

"Thank you, sir."

He waves his hand. "Stop with that sir bullshit. Call me Ray."

I nod, but don't say anything else. Something tells me he's not done talking yet.

"I know this is kinda last minute, but we'd love to hire you. You can tell us no. There is absolutely no pressure. We know you're busy working here, and it seems you've been keeping busy in your free time as well," he says, but doesn't say another word about the fact I'm spending said free time with his youngest daughter. "We'd love for you to make a small arch that can be used for the ceremony and then put in their backyard afterward in the landscaping."

I'm genuinely shocked by his request, but that's quickly replaced with a sense of honor. "I'd love to."

He seems a bit taken back by my instant agreement. "Yeah?"

"Absolutely. I'd be honored," I tell him, my mind already spinning ideas. "What do you have in mind?"

He shrugs. "We're leaving the creative part up to you."

"All right. I might send you a few photos to get an idea of what you're looking for."

Ray lifts his chin in thought. "Or you could ask Joy."

I open my mouth and close it quickly. "I could do that, if that's what you want."

Joy's father just smiles at me. "If you agree to make it, we're going to ask Eve is she has any preferences."

I feel like I just walked right into the comment about Joy. "Well, yes, I'll make it." The prospect of using Gramps's woodworking shed gets me all sorts of excited.

"Great," he replies, reaching over and giving me a thump on the back. "And as far as the other, she seems to be happy."

My eyes slowly connect with his as I swallow over the lump in my throat. "Uhh, I'm glad."

"Me too, son." He considers his words for a moment before adding, "Listen, it's none of my business, but for what it's worth, I thought you should know. I talked to her earlier this morning before I left for work. They were all headed to go dress shopping for the wedding, and even though we didn't talk about anything in particular, she just had this extra light about her, and she smiled nonstop. I think that probably has something to do with you, I assume?"

I try to keep my reaction neutral, but I can't. A grin spreads across my lips.

"I see she's not the only one," he states with a chuckle.

Clearing my throat, I meet his green eyes, the same ones both his daughters have, and say, "I'm enjoying spending time with your daughter."

He nods. "I think the feeling is mutual." Sobering, he adds, "You're planning to leave still?"

For the first time, I hesitate. I know what I need to say, but I struggle to get the words out. The thought of leaving still weighs heavy on my chest. "Yeah," I finally spit out, that one word like a hot knife to my insides.

"I know your life is back in South Carolina. You seem to have a great job, friends, and your immediate family there."

"I do," I reply. "But I also have some of that here too. Yes, my work and clients are back home, but I plan to keep in contact with my extended family and friends here."

"I hope you do." His smile is fatherly and warm, his eyes full of compassion and strength. "You have a place here too, Burk. Don't ever forget that."

My phone buzzes in my pocket, but I ignore it. Ray and I load the greenery into the bed of the side-by-side utility vehicle, his words hanging heavy between us. As soon as it's situated, my phone vibrates a second time.

Ray chuckles. "I'll take this up front. You go ahead and answer. It might be from someone important," he states with a wink, as if he knows it's his daughter messaging me.

When he walks away, I strip my gloves off my hands and retrieve the device. Joy's name lights up on the screen as I tap to read her message.

> **Joy:** Hope your day is going well. Mine is great! We all found dresses. Can't believe she's getting married in two weeks!

My fingers fly over the screen, desperate to respond.

> **Me:** I'm glad you found dresses, and it'll be here before you know it. Are you on your way back?

> **Joy:** Just got home. I'm heading down to the bakery to prep for tomorrow and make a grocery list. Wanna come over after you get off work?

> **Me:** How does pizza sound?

> **Joy:** Pizza always sounds good. It's a date.

> **Me:** Yes, it is. Sully's still the place to go?

> **Joy:** Affirmative.

I chuckle and shake my head at her silly reply.

> **Me:** Then, I'll grab dinner and meet you shortly.

> **Joy:** You remember what I like?

Me: Pepperoni with mushroom and onion.

Joy: You're good, my friend.

Me: No sausage.

Joy: Why would anyone put sausage on a pizza?!

Me: I don't share your sentiment, but I'll abide by your weird pizza topping wishes in hopes I can steal a few kisses later tonight.

Joy: Well, you keep talking like that and you might get more than just a few kisses.

Me: I'll bring you two pizzas.

Joy: *insert laughing emoji*

Me: Should be there around 6:30.

Joy: Back door will be unlocked. Come to the bakery.

Me: Lock the door, Easy-Bake. I'll knock.

Joy: Fine, but only because I don't want you to not bring pizza. Snowflake Falls is safe.

Me: And you will be too because the door will be locked.

Joy: See you soon. I'll be the one standing beneath the mistletoe.

Me: Three pizzas.

With a big, cheesy grin on my face, I place my phone back into my pocket and slip my gloves on. I have a little over two hours left of the workday, and then I'll secure my kiss, even if she's not standing beneath the mistletoe.

Before I even knock on the door, I test the knob to see if it's locked. It is, thankfully. No, I don't think she's in any real danger in Snowflake Falls, but the world isn't the same place it used to be, where you can leave your doors unlocked and go to bed without a care in the world.

I knock and hear the lock release just seconds later. Then, there she is, standing in the doorway looking like the most beautiful woman in the world on Christmas morning. "Hi."

Joy smiles. "Hi." Her gaze drops down to the pizza boxes in my hand. "Did you really bring three pizzas?"

I chuckle as she steps back and grants me entrance. "No, but I did bring a large pizza, some wings, and garlic breadsticks. I can't believe I've been here for almost two weeks and haven't had Sully's yet."

"That's because your grandma has been busy fattening you up," she replies, locking the back door behind us.

"Very true. She spent a little time this morning with Gramps, but then came home and worked the pay hut all afternoon. We were pretty busy," I state, setting the boxes on the counter because she's clearly been working at her big station in the middle of the room.

"Sorry, I haven't had time to clean up. Want to go upstairs?"

I glance around. "Why don't we move to the front and eat up there. You clearly have more work to do, and after I've fed you, I'll help."

Her eyebrows shoot upward. "You'll help?"

"I'm an excellent baker's assistant, Easy-Bake. I had plenty of practice as a boy."

"You ate the raw dough!" she bellows, grabbing two bottles of water from the fridge and following me up front.

"That's the most important job. Taste-tester. It's imperative to try both the before and after product."

She slips into the chair across from me, the sounds of her giggles filling the empty room. "If you say so. Now, you're not supposed to eat the raw dough because of eggs and whatnot."

I give her a pointed look, holding her gaze. "You still sample though, don't you?"

Her cheeks turn a beautiful shade of pink. "I do not."

"You do!" I proclaim through my laughter. "That's okay, I won't tell your secrets. I'm a vault."

She shakes her head, the grin still stretched across her gorgeous face. "I'm going to plead the fifth."

"Probably for the best," I state, opening the boxes and waiting for her to choose her food. "Dinner is served."

Just as I grab my first slice of pizza and add it to my plate with a breadstick and a couple of wings, my phone chimes. Usually, I'd ignore it and give the woman in front of me all my attention, but with everything going on with Gramps, I should at least check it to make sure it's not family.

As if sensing my hesitation, Joy says, "Go ahead and answer."

I pull out my phone and tap on the messaging app. I click on Ray's name and scan the message.

Ray: Eve and John would be honored to have you make an arch for their wedding. I'm attaching a photo of the altar area so you can get a visual. If you want to go in and take measurements, just say the word.

Me: Sounds good. I'll start drafting a design soon.

Ray: The bride and groom want it to be a surprise, so if you need any direction, Joy will help you.

Me: Sounds good. Thanks!

I snicker and flip my phone down on the table, picking up my pizza and taking a bite. "Sorry about that."

"Everything okay?" she asks, chowing down on a breadstick with cheddar cheese dipping sauce.

"Yes. That was your dad, actually."

That seems to catch her attention. "My dad? What did he want?"

"Your parents asked me to build an arch for the wedding. Something simple, not elaborate, that the happy couple can put in the landscaping in the backyard when it's all said and done."

Joy grins happily. "I love that."

"Your sister gave the go-ahead, but they're leaving the creative part up to me. They want to be surprised on their wedding day."

"Oh, I can't wait! Can I help?" she asks, practically vibrating in her seat.

"You want to help me build it?" I ask, trying to hide how turned on that thought makes me.

Her eyes are sparkling, and it has nothing to do with the decorations and lights covering every square inch of her bakery. "Yep. I've helped my dad do little things, but I've never actually taken a bunch of wood and helped build something from scratch."

"Well, you got it. Can you come to my grandparents' house tomorrow after work? I'm going to do some sketches and you can pick which one you think your sister would like the most."

"Oh my gosh, yes. I can't wait to help. Wait, you're going to let me do more than just pick a design, aren't you?" Her gorgeous green eyes narrow as she stares at me.

"Of course I am. You wanna help, then I'll let you help. My only rule is you end with the same number of fingers you started with."

That makes her giggle. "Deal. No way do I want to lose one of these puppies," she agrees, wiggling her fingers before reaching for her pizza.

"I'm quite partial to all ten of those too," I tease, leaving the innuendo hanging like the garland over the doorways. My memory is filled with recollections of feeling those fingers and her hands wrapped around the length of my cock after we woke up this morning.

Again, she blushes and diverts her gaze.

We finish eating, chatting about work and the upcoming holiday, and I realize I've never felt this content. This settled. This comfortable with a woman, especially one I've only been seeing a short period of time.

But that's the thing. I've known Joy my entire life, and being with her just feels...right.

After we clean up our pizza mess and place the leftovers in her refrigerator, I turn my attention her way. "What do you have left to do?"

"Well, I'm featuring hot cross buns with apricot jam and a fresh honey bun with honey glaze on my specialty menu this week, so I need to finish prepping the dough so it can rise overnight. I also need to make the eggnog buttercream frosting for my chocolate and spiced cupcakes."

I stop where I stand and give her my complete attention. "I know I just stuffed myself with pizza, but I could totally find room for a honey bun right now."

Joy giggles and moves to her workstation after washing her hands. "Well, they won't be ready until tomorrow morning, but I will save you one."

"Better make it two," I tell her, retrieving the stool and moving it toward where she works. "I can already tell I'm going to love them."

Shaking her head, she pulls out the recipe she's looking for and gets to work.

"Can I help?"

She looks up at me and grins. "Of course. Just make sure you finish up with the same number of fingers you started with."

Barking out a laugh, I move to the sink and scrub my hands with soap and water. Once they're dry, I stand beside her. "What should I do?"

Under her direction, I help make dough for tomorrow's pastries, and together, we follow that up with preparing the frosting. It smells amazing. I've always loved eggnog, even though I haven't had it in years prior to coming back to Snowflake Falls. In fact, I'm not sure I've had it since I left here all those years ago. It was a part of the holiday season, a tradition for everyone in town. When I left, the holidays had an entirely different look and feel, and I just don't remember having eggnog after we relocated.

Once it's ready to go, I remove the bowl from the big industrial mixer and offer the baker a grin. "I think it's good."

She nods and swipes her finger across the paddle attachment and slips it inside her mouth. "Oh my God, it's perfect."

I gape at her. "Do you know how long I've wanted to do that? But I was trying to be all sanitary and shit."

Joy giggles and shrugs her shoulders. "It's not like I just stuck my finger inside the bowl of frosting. The paddle will be cleaned next, so since it's not going to be used again, it's fine for a little sample."

Without asking for permission, I do exactly what she did. Only I don't take a tiny little sample. I slide my entire finger along the length of the paddle, gathering as much frosting as I can. The moment the sweetness hits my tongue, I moan in pleasure. "Damn, Joy. That's delicious."

"It is, isn't it." It's not a question, but a statement.

She quickly transfers the frosting to an airtight container and places it in the refrigerator. "Tomorrow morning, I'll have to let it return to room temperature and rewhip it, but the flavors will be even stronger thanks to leaving it to rest overnight."

"I'm gonna need one of those cupcakes with my honey buns," I tell her, taking another small swipe of frosting off the paddle.

"You're gonna have a sugar rush," she tells me, walking over to retrieve the bowl from where I stand.

As she grabs for it, I stop her. An idea forms in my head. "Leave it."

"For?" she asks, her cheeks turning a delightful shade of pink. We're standing very close together, and all I want to do is take her in my arms and have my wicked way with her.

"Dessert."

One eyebrow shoots upward in question.

"You, Easy-Bake," I reply, sliding my frosting-covered finger down her neck. I follow it with a long swipe of my tongue. The mixture of frosting and the taste of her skin sends all my blood south of my belt. "You're my dessert."

I'm about to put the frosting remnants to good use.

Chapter Seventeen

Joy

A shiver sweeps down my spine as he lazily drags his thumb across my lips. "What needs to be put away now?"

I glance at the workstation, even though I already know the answer. "Nothing." The dough is put in the refrigerator, and the rest of the dry ingredients are covered and can stay where they are. I always put refrigerated items away after using them, so I don't accidentally leave something out longer than I should, and even though I prefer to put everything away and clean, I have to admit, the temptation of leaving it until later is damn strong.

Burk is that temptation.

Lifting me up, I'm suddenly against his chest, my legs wrapped around his lower back. He gives me a cheeky grin and grabs the mixing bowl with his free hand. The other grips my ass, holding me tightly against him as he moves. "Everything's locked up down here, right?"

"It is," I state, giggling as he practically runs up the stairs to my apartment. It can't be easy, carrying me and the bowl and trying not to drop either, but he does it flawlessly.

Once we're inside my apartment, he carefully sets me down and turns, pinning me against the door. His eyes are pure fire, blazing with desire and need, and all I want to do is bathe in them. The bowl is set on the counter beside where we stand, and he reaches inside and uses his finger to scoop up more of the sweet icing.

"Hold still," he instructs, mischief dancing in those brown orbs.

I remain in place while he brushes frosting across my throat and lips. Then, his mouth descends, first cleaning my throat of all sweetness before he moves to my lips. I instantly open my mouth, allowing him to deepen the kiss. The frosting makes a huge mess on our faces, but neither of us seems to care.

He reaches for my sweater and lifts, tossing it onto the floor beside us. My bra goes next, and while I stand against the door, panting and pulling sweet oxygen into my lungs, he grabs more of the frosting from the bowl. It's cold as he glides his finger across each nipple, a devious smirk on his lips. "Dessert," he confirms before bending down and licking the treat off my body.

I arch my back, pressing my chest to his face as he continues to lick and suck. My fingers slide into his hair, gripping the strands and holding him in place. Pleasure courses through my veins, soaking my panties. A hum starts in my limbs and lands firmly between my legs.

Burk glances up without removing his mouth from my flesh. "Delicious."

I look over at the bowl on the counter. "You know, you could share."

A devilish smirk stretches slowly across his mouth. "What did you have in mind?"

Sliding my hands from his hair down his arms to grip the bottom of his shirt, I start to raise it up and say, "I believe you're not the only one who would enjoy licking a little frosting."

The rest of our clothes come off in record time, and before I know it, I'm standing naked in my kitchen staring at an equally naked gorgeous man. He's looking like he's ready to devour me from head to toe, with or without the frosting.

Reaching for my hand, he leads me farther into the kitchen and hoists me onto the counter. My legs wrap around his waist once more, but he shakes his head. "Here." He lifts one foot up and places it on the counter, spreading me open. His smile says it all.

I'm definitely his dessert.

My eyes are glued to him as he dips his finger inside the bowl and holds it up. He's meticulous as he brushes it across both nipples and then over my clit. Then, he devours. That's the only way to describe it. First, he licks the frosting off my nipples before turning his attention between my legs.

Burk flattens his tongue against my clit and slides it from bottom to top, clearing off the icing as he goes. But he doesn't stop there. In fact, he seems to double down his efforts, licking and sucking on the swollen bundle of nerves. When he shifts, he moves his hand, gliding his index finger through my wetness before pressing it inside my body.

Placing my hands on the counter behind me, I lean back as best I can, resting my head against the upper cabinet and giving him more room to continue. My hips start to roll as he pumps his finger in and out. He adds his middle finger, stretching me in the most glorious way possible. "Burk," I whisper through a gasp. I feel my body tightening like a coil as my release builds.

"You taste so fucking sweet," he murmurs against my flesh before delving deep inside my body. His fingers fuck me as the tips of those talented fingers curl upward, stroking that magical spot deep inside me. "I can tell you want to come, Joy."

I cry out, my orgasm so very close. "Yes."

He draws my clit between his lips and sucks hard, sending me flying over the edge. My release stretches on and on as his fingers and mouth draw out every last ounce I possess. When there's nothing left of me but a bone-deep sense of satedness, I slump back against the counter with my eyes closed and smile.

"I don't think I'd ever get tired of seeing you like this," he murmurs.

"Laid out on the counter?" I ask, cracking open my eyes to meet his.

"All naked and glowing after you came hard on my mouth." His smile is cocky. He's clearly proud of himself right now. Bringing his fingers to his lips, he draws them into his mouth and sucks. "I've never tasted anything sweeter. You're the ultimate sugar rush."

Warmth spreads through my chest, and suddenly, all I want to do is return the favor. I need to bring him to his knees—figuratively, of course—just like he so effortlessly does to me.

Carefully, I get up, and when Burk notices I'm climbing off the counter, he's there to help me. As soon as my feet hit the floor, I reach for his cock. It's hard and ready, jetting straight out toward me. Licking my lips, I gently stroke him from root to tip as I move the bowl closer to where I stand.

Turnabout is fair play, Mr. Whitman.

Swiping my finger through the frosting, I run it over the head of his cock and down the shaft. I feel him shiver as he watches me, his eyes riveted in place. Dropping to my knees, I wrap my hand around him once more and move forward. I swirl my tongue over the tip, tasting the sweet frosting.

"Fuck," Burk mumbles.

Gazing up at his wide brown eyes, I slowly draw the length of him into my mouth as far as I can. He physically sucks in a deep breath, and his entire body goes rigid. He holds perfectly still as I gently pick up speed. I alternate between swirling my tongue around the head of his cock and sucking as hard and deep as I can. Burk moves his hands to my hair and wraps one hand around my ponytail. He doesn't pull or force me to do anything, just holds on.

With my eyes locked on his, I gently start to twist my hand as I work him over. I relax my throat and bob up and down, sucking him deeper into my throat.

A loud groan fills my kitchen as his hand tightens around my hair. It doesn't hurt. If anything, it throws fuel on an already raging fire. Even though my knees hurt and I'm losing feeling in my arm, I keep my focus on giving him as much pleasure as possible. Reaching down with my other hand, I cup his balls and apply even more suction. The result is exactly what I was hoping for.

Burk thrusts his hips and groans, muttering something about my mouth. "I'm gonna come. If you don't want it down your pretty throat, back away now."

I don't move and keep bobbing my head and massaging his balls. He rocks his hips and grips my hair before stilling completely. I feel the first powerful surge of cum before he starts to move again. He pumps into my mouth until he has nothing left and sags against the counter behind him.

"Wow," he mutters, releasing his hold on my hair.

When I stand up and wipe my mouth, he pulls me into his strong arms and gingerly runs his hand over my head. "Did I hurt you?"

"No," I confirm, gazing up at him through my eyelashes. "I liked it."

He presses his lips to mine in a firm, chaste kiss. "I did too. Thank you."

"No need to thank me. I believe it was mutually enjoyable."

He snorts and grins. "Do you need to do anything else or are you done for the night?"

"I'm done," I confirm. Everything downstairs can wait until tomorrow morning.

"Good," he replies, picking me up and heading for the door. He flicks the lock before stalking toward my bedroom. "It's almost bedtime, but first," he says, kissing my neck as we move. "First, we need to shower."

Even though the holidays are my most favorite time of the year, in my line of work, they can also be overwhelming and stressful. I've reached my max on outside orders and even added a few extras to my calendar because I felt bad for telling people no before Christmas. Between helping my sister with wedding plans and working all day and into the evening at the bakery, I've barely been able to spend quality time with Burk. Sure, he's come over and helped me clean the bakery and prepare for the next day, and I've even stolen some time to go over to his grandpa's woodshop and help make my sister's arch, but it feels so rushed. We fall into bed together at the end of the day, only to get up before the sun and start the process all over again.

Tomorrow is Christmas Eve, which means this is my final night to complete customer orders. Burk is with his grandma, preparing for his grandpa's release from the rehab center. I'm super excited for them all, especially Dale. His goal was to get his strength back enough to be home for Christmas, and he'll do it. He's supposed to be released tomorrow morning.

I'm using my free time to finish my sister's wedding cake. It's a small chocolate cake with eggnog buttercream frosting. Apparently, John had one of my cupcakes last week and decided it would make the perfect wedding cake for them to share at the reception. I have to agree. It's a decadent combination of rich mocha chocolate and holiday-infused frosting.

I check my phone for the umpteenth time and push it aside when I don't see any notifications. I know Burk is busy with family, but he said he'd text me when he was on his way back to Snowflake Falls. It's getting late, and to be honest, I would have thought he'd be back by now. They have a big day tomorrow when he's released, so I assumed they'd want to get back and get some rest.

Knowing there's nothing left for me to do tonight, I carefully transport my sister's final cake to the fridge, where it'll be kept until Christmas. Just as I close the door and exhale the breath I was holding, I hear a distant knock on the entrance. Turning, I move in the direction of the noise and step into the front side of the bakery.

Under the streetlights, I see Burk standing on the other side of the door, a wide smile on his face. Moving toward him, I release the lock on the door and pull it open. "What are you doing? I thought you were going to text me."

He steps inside the bakery, gently shaking his head and sending flakes of fresh snow falling to the floor. "I wanted to surprise you. These are for you." He extends his hand, holding up the gorgeous bouquet of red roses.

I slip my nose into the blooms and inhale the sweet floral scent. "They're gorgeous, thank you," I proclaim, offering a wide smile.

Burk presses his lips to mine. "That's not the only surprise. Can you take a walk with me?"

I glance back toward the kitchen area and mentally run through what I have out and left to clean. Realizing there isn't much left, I reply, "I need to put the leftover frosting in the fridge, but that's about it."

His eyes turn molten instantly. "Frosting, huh?"

A giggle slides easily from my lips as I shake my head. "Sorry, no can do. I need what's left for cupcakes in the morning."

Together, we walk into the kitchen. The moment he crosses the threshold, he stops. "Wow."

I turn and follow his line of sight. It's the first time I really take in the scene. I have a large shelving unit I use for custom orders, and it's completely full. Not to mention the far counter is stacked and the fridge is packed. Cakes, cupcakes, pies, specialty breads, cookies, and everything in between. I've had a busy few days, as evident by the amount of white pastry boxes containing my baked goods.

"This is my busiest time of year," I tell him, moving to the cabinet and retrieving a vase. I don't receive flowers often, but it has happened on occasion. After arranging the roses in the vase and adding water, I place the fragrant blooms on the counter near the cash register.

"All done?" Burk asks, his eyes sparkling with excitement.

Nodding, I move to the container of frosting and place it in the fridge. "Done."

"Come on," he says, extending his hand.

I place mine in his willingly. "What do I need?" I ask when I realize he's not leading me upstairs.

"Coat, gloves, and hat."

I give him a quick look of wonder before moving to the back door to retrieve my winterwear. After slipping it all on, I go ahead and stuff my feet into my snow boots because something tells me I'm going to need those too. When I'm ready to step outside, I turn my attention to the man who makes my heartbeat quicken and my panties a little damp. "Ready."

He flashes a quick grin and reaches for my hand.

We walk through the bakery, grabbing my phone and keys off the counter and flipping off the lights as I go. When we step outside, I lock the door and face Burk. "Now what?"

"Now, we walk," he confirms, reaching down and picking up a duffel bag left beside the front door.

"Where are we walking to?" I ask, taking in the freshly fallen snow and the mostly quiet streets of downtown.

"Not far. It's a beautiful night."

I glance up, a soft smile stretching across my lips. "It is." The moon is full and high in the sky, giving off enough light that if the streetlights weren't in play, you could still see your surroundings. "What's in the bag?"

His answer is a cheeky grin, one that makes me chuckle. "Fine. Keep your secrets."

"It won't be a secret for long. Come on," he says, leading me across the street toward the town square. When we reach the pavilion near the skating rink, he stops. "Wait here." Setting the bag down on a picnic table, he kisses my knuckles before releasing my hand then takes off running. I watch until he disappears around the back of the utility building toward the edge of the park.

Suddenly, the lights come on. A million white twinkle lights illuminate the night around me and soft holiday music is piped through the speakers. My jaw drops open as I take in the scene, one I've experienced so many times before, but am seeing it for the first time with no one around.

Burk returns, a smile on his handsome face. "Surprise." He reaches for his bag and pulls out my ice skates.

"What? How—"

"I stole them yesterday morning when I left to go back to my grandparents' house."

Shaking my head, I take the offered skates and have a seat on the bench. "So, you've been planning this."

"I have," he boasts proudly, pulling a second set of skates from the bag and getting to work putting them on. "I even borrowed skates from Klint."

When we're both wearing skates and smiles, we make our way to the rink, which has been freshly cleaned of any snow. We step onto the ice, and he immediately takes my hand. "How did you pull this off?" I ask curiously.

"Well, turns out Jim McMillian still takes care of the park. I ran into him at the tree farm the other day and ran my idea by him, which might have included a donation to the town park fund to help seal the deal."

I look up and close my eyes. The cold air mixed with the warmth of his hand wrapped around mine, something I feel even through gloves, and the glow of Christmas lights is something that will forever be embedded in my mind when I think back on this night. It's perfect.

"This is the most romantic thing anyone has ever done for me," I confess as we move around the ice.

"Yeah?" he asks, a glint of pride reflecting in his eyes.

"Definitely. You've combined my favorite things. Roses, ice skating under the twinkle lights, holiday music, and you."

Suddenly, he stops and pulls me into his arms. My breathing hitches as his gaze lands on my lips. I wet them quickly with my tongue, a movement he catches sight of if the dilation of his eyes is any indication. "Can I kiss you?"

"Yes, please."

It starts gentle but quickly turns heated. His tongue delves deep inside my mouth, tasting and teasing in the best way possible. Every problem or stress of the day falls away as we stand in the middle of the ice-skating rink and make out like teenagers. It's exactly what I've needed after a very long day.

When we finally pull apart, wet flakes of snow start to fall onto our faces. We both look up and smile. It's like a Christmas movie or a holiday card come to life, and I'm here, standing in the middle of the magic. It's the icing on top of the Christmas cupcake.

The sugar rush after eating the most decadent dessert ever.

His gloved hand comes up to cup my cheek as he brushes his warm lips across mine once more. "Come on, Easy-Bake. Let's skate."

Chapter Eighteen

Burk

"Merry Christmas," my grandparents holler the moment I come down the stairs to join them for coffee in the kitchen.

"Merry Christmas," I reply, bending down to kiss Gram's cheek and squeezing Gramps' shoulder. "You two are up early."

"We wanted to see the sunrise together over the tree farm," Gram informs me, smiling behind her coffee mug.

"It's good to be home," Gramps confirms, reaching for his wife's hand and linking their fingers.

I stop in my tracks, staring down at their hands. They've aged over the years, but they're still the same hands they've held for the last fifty years. My grandparents built this farm and a life together. They grew from a young married couple to what they are now. I'm envious of their love, their commitment, and maybe it's because for the first time in my life, I truly want what they have.

Clearing my throat, I move to the coffee maker and pour myself a mug. I add just a splash of creamer and a bit of sugar and join them at the table. I look at the basic coffee and already miss Joy. Even though I messaged her first thing this morning and wished her a Merry Christmas, I wish she were right beside me, sharing some of her delicious coffee creations that will give me cavities and a sugar rush.

I want her beside me, holding my hand, and watching the sunrise.

"How are you feeling?" I ask Gramps.

"Never been better," he assures me with a wide smile. You can still see a hint of a droop on the right corner of his mouth. He's physically doing well, but there's still a few characteristics of his stroke he'll most likely always have. "Nothing better than waking up on Christmas morning with the woman you love back in the home you built together." He gazes lovingly at my grandma. It's so powerful, I have to look away.

"I'm glad you're home."

Gramps clears his throat. "I hear you've kept yourself busy in my shop."

I nod. "I hope that's okay."

His brown eyes widen with delight. "Are you kidding me? I've been wanting someone to share in the joy of woodworking for as long as I can remember. Your uncle Karl used to tinker a bit, but never really got into it like I did. And your dad, well, it was never his thing."

I hold his gaze and confirm, "It wasn't."

He clears his throat once more and takes a sip of his coffee. "I was sitting outside, watching the sunrise, and just couldn't get over how beautiful of a view I had. It's something I'll never take for granted, Burk. But as I was watching that sun come up with renewed vision, I realized not everyone shared my views." He levels me with a sad look as he adds, "And that's okay. I've made a lot of mistakes in my life, and this morning, I took the first step to apologize. I called your dad."

Shock sweeps through me as I look across the table at the older man who resembles my own father so much. "You did?"

He nods. "I did. What's more surprising is he answered."

That makes me smile. "I'm glad."

"Me too, though I wouldn't have been surprised if he hadn't. But he did, and I was able to wish him and your mom a Merry Christmas. We actually talked for about thirty minutes."

My heart feels lighter now, happier.

"Anyway, we've both agreed to open up the lines of communication. We'll both stay in contact and, hopefully, rebuild the relationship we broke." When he looks my way, there are tears in his eyes. Happy ones. Taking another drink of his coffee, he says, "Tell me about what you've been doing in the shop."

So, I do. I tell him about building the arch for John and Eve's wedding later tonight. I took it to the church yesterday so it could be decorated. From what I was told by Ray, they'll wrap it in fresh holiday greenery and flowers before the ceremony, and even though it's not the first one I've built, I'm more excited to see this one complete and serving its purpose than any other I've made in the past.

"It's a beautiful day for a wedding," Gram states.

"It is. Are you sure you two don't want to come? I'm more than happy to chauffeur you around." I know my grandparents were invited as friends of Ray and Cindy's, but with Gramps being recently released from the rehab center, they've decided to stay home and rest.

Gram grins and shakes her head. "We appreciate the offer, but we'll be all set here. I have a card for the happy couple, if you'd deliver it to them for us."

"Of course I will."

"Thank you." Gram drinks her coffee and asks, "When are you doing your gift exchange with Joy?"

I glance over at the wrapped box sitting near the tree. I added it last night, after finally finishing the contents. It took me way longer than normal, but mostly because I just didn't have a lot of free time to work on it. When I was in the shop, Joy was with me, helping finish the arch for her sister's wedding, and most of my nights the last two weeks have been spent with Joy wrapped in my arms in her bed.

"Tonight. Their family is doing a small gift exchange this morning at breakfast, and then they'll spend the rest of the day preparing for the wedding." Joy invited me over to her family's gathering, but I didn't want to leave my grandparents this morning. It's Gramps's first full day back home, and I wanted to share that with him. She understood completely, which is why we agreed to do our exchange later tonight, after the small reception.

"Well, she's going to love it. I mean, I don't know what it is, but if you built it, I'm certain it's a beautiful piece full of meaning," Gram says.

"Thank you. I hope she likes it." I think about what's in the box and how I came up with the idea. I won't say a word about everything that transpired between Joy and myself the night the idea formed. Those moments, which started in her kitchen and ended with us naked upstairs in her apartment, are just for me.

Once I leave, they'll be some of my most treasured memories.

A knot forms in my gut. Actually, it's not a new knot, but one I've felt grow steadily over the last week as my time in Snowflake Falls winds down. As the hourglass sand starts to run out and I think about leaving, that knot tightens, making it hard to breathe.

Before we can continue our conversation, chaos erupts at the door. "Merry Christmas," my uncle Karl bellows as he enters the house, followed closely by his wife, Sheila, as well as Klint, Gretchen, Noah, and Tasha. They're loaded down with gifts, as well as delicious smelling food for our breakfast together.

I stand up and help take boxes and gift bags, delivering them to the tree while everyone removes their boots and coats. I'm pulled into a tight hug from my aunt Sheila, as well as from Klint's wife, Gretchen. My youngest cousin, Tasha, walks over and gives me a fist bump, while little Noah runs over to my leg and gives me a hug and toothy grin, and yells, "Merry Christmas!"

This is home. This is family. Yes, I miss my parents. They should be here, celebrating with everyone else. Maybe someday they'll get to that point again. I truly hope it happens.

As the noise level increases and everyone gives Gramps a little extra attention, I catch movement out of the corner of my eye. I lift my arm and pull my Gram against my side. Her familiar arms wrap around my waist as she rests her head against my chest. "I'm so glad you're here, Burk." There are tears in her eyes as she looks up at me.

"Me too," I assure her, feeling my own eyes burn with emotion.

"You're always welcome here. Always."

I give her a smile and press a kiss to her forehead. "I know."

"Good. Now, I'm going to say something else I think you need to hear. I know I'm probably overstepping my bounds, but I think it's important." She levels me with a gaze full of love as she says, "If you love her, make sure she knows. Even if you return home afterward as planned, don't let the words go unsaid. They're too important, too meaningful not to say them."

My throat closes and I find it hard to draw air into my lungs. "I will."

She nods. "Good, because that woman deserves to feel your love and hear you say the words."

"I promise I'll tell her." There's sadness in my voice.

She cups my cheek with her hand and offers her own sad smile. "One day at a time, Burk. That's all you can do. And maybe, someday down the road, the day will come when you return to Snowflake Falls.

Return to her. But even if that day doesn't come, she'll be okay. You will be too. Because love doesn't just die when you leave someone. It's always there, deep inside you. Your heart just continues to grow and make room for more love. It's one of the most beautiful, yet painful parts of life."

I know she's talking about more than just me and Joy. She lost her son, daughter-in-law, and grandson the day my family's pride ripped through us. Like a photograph, it was torn in two, separating us into two sides. Gram kept in touch with my dad, mom, and me the best she could, but it was difficult. There was still tension, and it was felt by everyone.

"You're a very wise woman, you know that?" I state, needing to lighten the mood a little.

She giggles and grins. "I do know that. I like to remind your grandfather of that point on many occasions."

I bark out a laugh. "As you should."

She keeps her arm wrapped around my waist as she pulls me toward the kitchen, where my family is gathered. "Come on, let's eat."

I pull open the heavy wooden door and step inside the small chapel. What I see when I enter is nothing short of beautiful. The old stone fireplace straight ahead is glowing with warmth and there are a combination of white twinkle lights and fresh flowers everywhere. The room feels like Christmas, mixed with elegance and love, and I'm honored to be included.

Movement catches out of the corner of my eye and I look to my right. When I do, my heart stops beating. My jaw drops and I struggle to do something as simple as breathing. The most exquisite creature in the world is standing there, smiling.

"Hi."

I run my hand over my mouth and try to catch my bearings. "Hello," I reply, taking a few steps toward her. "You look...wow."

Joy smiles, her deep-red lipstick the same color as the dress she's wearing. "You look very handsome," she states, taking in my dark denim jeans, black button-down dress shirt, and deep red tie. Funny I chose this tie from Gramps's closet without knowing what color dress Joy would be wearing. She steps forward and grabs the silk tie, gently running her fingers down the material. "Doesn't it look magnificent?" she asks, turning her gaze to the small chapel.

My eyes, however, stay glued to her. "Breathtaking."

As if feeling my eyes on her, she glances my way and smiles. "I was talking about the church."

"I know, and I was talking about you."

"Burk!"

Before I can take Joy into my arms and smear that red lipstick all over my face, we're interrupted by Joy's dad, Ray. "Good to see you, sir," I greet, extending my hand for a shake.

"Hey, hey, now none of that, remember?" I nod. "Good. Glad you could come tonight. How's your grandpa doing?"

"Very well, thank you. He's happy to be back home," I confirm, noticing that Joy shifts to standing directly beside me. Without taking my gaze off her dad, I reach down and slip my fingers around hers.

"I'm sure he is. Cindy and I plan to stop by tomorrow for a quick visit," he says with a jovial smile.

"They'll appreciate that."

He slaps me on the back of the shoulder and gives it a squeeze. "Good to see you. I'm about to go have my first view of the bride and prepare to walk her down the aisle." He looks at his youngest daughter and smiles. "I'll see you in there in a few minutes."

Joy nods and accepts a kiss on her cheek from her dad. When he leaves us alone, stepping inside one of the closed doors to the side of the space, she returns her attention to me. "I should get back in there. The ceremony will be starting soon."

I bring our linked hands to my mouth and place a kiss on her knuckles. "I'll see you in a bit."

She goes up on her tiptoes as she leans in for a kiss. I oblige willingly, wishing we were alone so I could ravish her. That would probably be frowned upon in the middle of a church on Christmas Day, so I keep my actions PG and break the kiss before I can act on the inappropriate thoughts plaguing my brain.

I watch as she walks away, entering through the same doorway her dad went just a short bit ago. When the door is closed soundly behind her, I turn my attention to the church. Instantly, I recognize almost everyone here. John, the groom, is standing in the middle of the main aisle, smiling and shaking hands with everyone who enters.

As I approach, he turns his attention my way. "Burk, glad you could join us."

"Appreciate the extended invite."

"We don't have sides, but I believe Ray and Cindy asked for you to sit behind them," John informs me, surprising me with the gesture.

John walks toward the front of the church and points to a pew. "Ariel is going to join you in a few minutes. I believe she's in with my bride. Oh, and thank you for making the arch. It's absolutely beautiful work."

"You're very welcome. I was happy to do it." I slip into the pew and move toward the end to ensure there's plenty of room for anyone else. I feel odd sitting so close to the front, especially when there are other people who are close to the bride and groom. I'm just Joy's friend, but even as I think that, it doesn't sit right. I'm her friend, yes, but my heart screams for more.

I *am* more than just a friend.

I'm the man who fell in love with her.

Soft instrumental Christmas music fills the room as everyone takes a seat. My eyes are pulled to the back of the room as Ariel exits the small room housing the bride and makes her way toward me. She pauses, giving John a hug and a kiss on the cheek before sliding into the pew. "Hi, Burk," she greets.

"Ariel, good to see you again," I tell her.

All eyes move to the back of the chapel as John escorts his mom and grandma down the aisle. He leads them to the front, directly behind where he will be standing, and gives them both a big hug and kiss on the cheek. Next, he returns to the back and offers an arm to Cindy, Joy and Eve's mom. He does the same for her, escorting her to the other front pew and accepting a big hug from his future mother-in-law.

Then, he walks to the altar, directly in front of the arch I made for them and turns his attention to the back of the room. His old friend, Linus McCaffrey, joins him as his best man, and together, they wait for the bride.

My eyes are drawn to the back of the room, as if sensing Joy's appearance. She steps out of the room, wearing a beaming smile and tears in her eyes as she slowly makes her way to the front of the chapel. She glances my way and winks before stepping opposite Linus and watching for her sister's arrival.

The music changes to "The Wedding March," and everyone inside the small church stands. On the arm of her father, Eve steps into the chapel and walks toward John. While the bride is absolutely stunning, I find myself looking toward the groom. To the man who is about to commit his life and love to this one woman for the rest of his life. Envy fills my soul, not because of who he has, but simply what.

He has the woman he loves for the rest of his life.

My eyes move to Joy, who has tears streaming down her face as she watches her sister approach the groom. There's so much happiness radiating off her, so much love for her big sister, I can feel it all the way over here.

She deserves this.

She deserves to be loved.

She deserves to hear me say the words.

I'll be honest, I don't really pay much attention to the ceremony. I'm focused on the maid of honor. I memorize everything about her, the curve of her body, the way her hair frames her face, the way she bites down on her bottom lip when she's trying to hold back more tears. The way she smiles at John when he's reciting his vows to Eve. I take it all in, committing every single detail to memory. In fifty years, I may not be able to recall the wedding, but I'll be damned sure I'll recollect everything about Joy Campbell.

Every. Fucking. Thing.

I realize in this moment I want Joy.

I want her tomorrow.

I want her forever, if she'll have me.

There's no way I can leave her. It would be equivalent to cutting my heart from my chest and walking away from it. I can't—no, I won't do it.

Now, I just have to figure out how to tell her.

And hope she feels the same way.

Chapter Nineteen

Joy

"You're in love with him."

I pull my gaze away from Burk, who is standing in the dining room with my dad, and turn to the familiar voice of my sister. My mouth opens, but no words come out. I can't deny it. It would be a lie if I did, so why do it?

"It's okay, you don't have to say anything. I see it on your face. It's written in your eyes."

I sigh and give my sister my complete attention. "I don't want him to go." I feel tears coming, and I do everything in my power to keep them at bay.

"Of course you don't," she replies gently. "Because you love him."

I sniffle, blinking rapidly to keep the wetness from falling. "I don't know what to do."

"Tell him."

I let out a deep breath. "I can't, Eve. He's leaving soon, returning to the other side of the country. What good will it do to confess how I feel?"

"It would give him all the pieces to the puzzle, Joy. If he knows all the facts, maybe he'll consider staying."

"He has a life there. A home, a business, friends. His parents are there."

"But you're here," she adds gently. "I can't tell you what to do or say, but I think you should tell him how you feel. Then, if he decides he's still going home, then that's on him. You gave him the choice. Right now, he doesn't know that you're desperately in love with him and probably always have been."

"Why would he stay, Eve? I mean, just because I tell him I love him doesn't mean he should move back here."

"Why not?"

I sigh and shake my head. "Because what if he moves here and we give it a go, and we end up breaking up? What if it doesn't work out?"

She swipes at a piece of hair hanging across my forehead before she whispers, "What if it does?"

My heart climbs up into my throat, making it hard to breathe. I blink away more tears, trying to remain calm and not let my emotions get the better of me.

"There's my wife. Come share a dance with me," John says as he takes my sister's hand and leads her to the center of the family room.

The entire house is covered in head-to-toe Christmas, and even though Eve and I didn't grow up in a huge home, there's plenty of room to host a small gathering of less than two dozen people. We've enjoyed cake and champagne and now my sister and her husband are sharing their first dance. Surrounded by Christmas lights, decorated trees, and their closest family and friends, it's the perfect way to finish out their wedding day.

"Well, hello there, beautiful." Burk steps up behind me and wraps his hand around my waist, drawing my back to his chest. He presses a light kiss on the side of my head and starts to sway to the music.

"Hello, yourself." I lean against his body, reveling in the way he feels against me. I close my eyes, letting the music wrap around me, and just...feel.

"Dance with me, beautiful."

I open my eyes and realize there are other couples dancing with the bride and groom in the middle of the living room. Placing my hand in his, I let Burk lead me out with the others and pull me into his arms. We move to the beat of the song, and a few tears silently slide down my cheeks. The mixture of the beautiful Christmas music, being wrapped in his arms, and surrounded by those I hold nearest and dearest to my heart is too much for my fragile emotional state.

"Hey, what's wrong?" Burk asks, placing a finger beneath my chin and gently lifting my face. The sadness in his eyes reflects that in mine, and it's almost too much.

"I'm just—" I clear my throat and do my best to get myself under control. "I'm just emotional, I suppose. It was a beautiful day. I'm so happy for my sister and John."

He gives me a small smile. "It was definitely a beautiful day, and while I'm certain it was perfect for the bride and groom, my favorite part is this right now. Dancing with the most beautiful woman in the world."

I lose the fight. His words are too much for my delicate psyche. I lean my cheek against his chest and silently cry, wishing things could be different between us. Wishing my love for him would be enough to make him stay.

Burk doesn't say a word, just holds me even tighter as the tears fall. Even after the song ends, he doesn't let go and we dance to the next one too. When that song ends, he places his thumb and index finger on my chin and lifts my face. "You ready to get out of here?"

I nod, feeling drained and numb. The ache in my chest is consuming, like a wildfire destroying everything in its path. If I'm going to completely fall apart, I want to do it in the privacy of my own home, not in front of my family. I swipe quickly at my tears and paste a smile on my lips.

Burk keeps a firm grasp on my hand as he leads me to where my parents are standing and watching their oldest daughter dance with her new husband. "I'm feeling a little tired, so I think we're going to head out," I tell them as I approach.

"Of course, dear," Mom replies, pulling me in for a hug. "John and Eve are getting ready to head to that bed-and-breakfast for the night and will join us for lunch tomorrow."

My parents gifted them with an overnight stay at a private cabin at a bed-and-breakfast not too far out of town. It's quite popular with the tourists, and when the owner found out Eve and John were getting married on Christmas, they insisted they use that particular cabin so they have more privacy.

"I'll be here," I tell her.

Then, I turn my attention to my dad, who wraps me in his arms and holds me tightly. He kisses me on the side of the head, and whispers, "Tell him, honey. I think he feels the same."

I close my eyes, praying he's right. Because if I say the words I long to say and he doesn't feel the same, it would kill a piece of my soul. "Love you."

"Love you more, honey." He kisses my forehead before turning his attention to Burk. He extends his hand. "Take care of my baby."

"Always," Burk replies, shaking my dad's hand firmly.

I try not to read too much into his words, instead giving my attention to my sister. She glances over and offers a small smile and a wave. I return the gesture, blowing her a kiss before making my way to the front door. Burk helps me slip on my winter coat and grabs his as well before taking my hand and leading me out of the house.

He presses the remote start button on the key fob on his rental and escorts me that way. When we left the small church where the ceremony was held, I rode with Burk, since my vehicle was left at home. After Mom did our hair at the salon, Eve and I rode with her to the church to get ready. It was easier that way.

Burk helps me into the passenger side of his rental and closes the door behind me. I try to take a few moments to calm my racing heart, but it's no use. I'm too worked up right now, especially knowing the end is near. In a couple of days, Burk will be flying back to South Carolina, his return to Snowflake Falls a complete unknown.

When he climbs inside, he reaches for my hand and links our fingers together. We ride back to my place without saying a word. The air is so thick with everything unspoken. It's almost hard to breathe.

By the time we pull into the alleyway behind the bakery and he parks, I think I've finally gotten myself calm enough to not burst into another fit of tears the moment we walk through the door. My movements are almost robotic as I climb from the vehicle and pull my keys from my small clutch purse. I don't even realize my fingers are shaking until Burk wraps his hand around them and stops me.

Gently, he takes the keys from my hand and unlocks the door, pushing it open and waiting for me to step through. The moment we're inside, the door is relocked behind us and we're making our way up the steps. The upper door is unlocked too, and we're finally inside my small apartment.

Burk sets down a duffel bag before moving to the tree. He turns on the lights and sets a box down in front of it. There's only one other present left, and that's the one I got for him. We agreed to do our exchange tonight, but now, I don't feel jovial or anxious to give him the gift I spent so much time and energy making.

"Come here," he says, taking off his coat and dropping it onto the couch. I do the same and go willingly to where he's standing in front of the tree.

Once I reach his side, he pulls me into his arms and hugs me tightly. I don't know how long we stay right here embracing, but it feels like forever, yet not long enough at the same time.

Pulling back, he cups my cheeks in his big hands and brushes his lips across mine. "Come on, let's open presents."

We move to the couch, sitting side by side in front of the brightly lit tree. Even with the hundreds of lights adorning it, my Christmas tree just feels like it lost its luster. I can't help but wonder if I'll ever look at it and feel peace and joy ever again, or will it remind me of the man I love and lost?

"Here," he says proudly, smiling brightly as he hands me the wrapped box.

I push aside the pain and focus on the now as I remove the bow and tear into the paper. I can't help but notice it contains a family ice-skating and enjoying other holiday traditions on the thick paper.

Ripping open the box, I push aside the red and green tissue paper and pull the wooden object out. My eyes tear up when I realize what it is. It's a tabletop cookbook holder. Not just any cookbook holder. One Burk handmade with two words etched on the base.

Easy-Bake.

Happy tears stream down my face as I run my hand over the intricate carvings and details of the nickname he gave me all those years ago.

He glides his rough thumb over the apple of my cheeks and swipes away the fresh tears. "I love it," I whisper, the words barely audible.

He gives me a small smile. "Good. After I saw you pull that cookbook out and prop it against something on your workstation, I knew what I had to make you."

I sniffle and reach for the shirt box wrapped beneath the tree. "Here. It's not as amazing as this is though," I tell him, holding onto this fantastic, thoughtful gift as if it were a lifeline.

Burk digs right into the present, sending scraps of paper flying and making me giggle. He looks like a four-year-old ripping into the gift with so much anticipation and excitement, it's hard not to feel that kind of joy.

When he opens the lid and pulls out the gift, he seems to stop breathing. All he does is stare down at the item I made him. Or more specifically, the photograph it contains. He looks up at me, his eyes wide with shock. "Where did you find this picture?"

I glance at the frame and offer a small grin. "Mom was going through photos a week ago and she stumbled on it. It was mixed in with all the Christmas pictures from that year. She thinks we were probably ten when she took it."

His eyes drop once more to the captured memory of two little kids who were the best of friends. A boy and girl ice-skating around the rink during the annual festival, the lights twinkling around them as they both smile widely for the camera.

"You made this." Burk runs his fingers across the smooth wooden frame.

"I did," I confirm, clearing my throat. "I know it's not as good as one you'd be able to make, probably with your eyes closed, but I enjoyed making it for you."

"How? When?" he asks, his brown eyes full of wonder.

"Last week, after Mom found the photograph. I took some of the thin pieces of scrap wood when I was helping you clean up your grandpa's shop after you finished building the arch. I took them to my dad, and he helped me make the frame. I did most of it myself, thanks to the knowledge you shared when we built the arch."

He beams proudly. "You did a great job."

"I didn't, but I figured it was more the sentiment than the actual gift."

"No, don't sell yourself short, Joy. This is amazing. I love it," he insists, leaning forward and pressing his lips to mine.

I ignore the way my heart skips a beat when he tells me he *loves* the gift I made him. If only he was using that word in a different context.

He sighs and sits back, putting space between us. "Do you want to take a walk?"

His question surprises me a bit, considering we haven't been inside too long. "Oh, uh, okay?"

Standing up, he extends his hand toward me and helps me rise. We gather our coats and slip stocking caps on our heads. I glance down at my dress shoes and know they won't keep my feet warm for any length of time outside, so I grab one of the thick pairs of wool socks I keep by my washer and dryer and slip those on my feet. Once they're in place, I slide my winter boots on and turn my attention to Burk.

"Should I change out of my dress?" I ask, glancing down at the deep-red floor-length dress I'm wearing beneath my winter coat.

He just smiles. "I'll keep you warm."

My cheeks flush as images of him doing just that filter through my brain. "Are you going to put on boots?" I ask, looking down at his black shoes.

"I'll be all right, Easy-Bake. Besides, we won't be out for long."

I nod, indicating I'm ready, so he takes my hand and leads me down the steps. I don't bother to lock the door, hoping we really won't be gone long. I just can't imagine someone breaking into my place on Christmas night.

Together, we walk outside and toward the end of the buildings, making our way to the park in the middle of town. Despite being forecast, it hasn't snowed today, so the sidewalks are still fairly clean, as are the roadways. We cross at the light and make our way to the walkway through the middle of the town square. The lights are still on, a million white lights illuminating the area, giving off the perfect Christmas glow.

"Here." Burk stops walking and turns to face me. He has both of my bare hands tucked inside his, keeping them warm and us anchored together.

I glance around, trying to figure out what's going on. No one is around. We're literally standing in the middle of the sidewalk, surrounded by the calm of Christmas. "What's going on?"

He takes a deep breath. "I have something I want to say to you, and I wanted to do it here." He looks around, a faint smile stretching across his lips. "This is one of the places I have the most memories of my time in Snowflake Falls. Every single one of those memories features you."

My own grin breaks out across my face. "We spent a lot of time together when we were little."

"We did."

Reaching up, he runs his thumb across my chin and cheek. "I'm leaving the day after tomorrow."

That's when the rug gets pulled out beneath my feet.

That's when my heart breaks.

Chapter Twenty

Burk

I can tell by the devastation that sweeps across her gorgeous face she thinks I'm preparing to say goodbye. And I am, but that's not all.

Hating the look on her face, I brush my lips across hers, closing my eyes and reveling in the feel of the connection. "I love you," I whisper, finally speaking the words I've longed to say.

Her entire body tenses moments before her eyes slowly open. Green eyes gaze up at me, stunned by my admission. "You love me?"

"Yeah," I reply with a small smile. "I think I always have."

Kissable lips form a little O as she stares up at me. "But…you're leaving," she finally says after a bit of hesitation.

"Yeah," I reply, wrapping my arms firmly around her and making sure she's as close as she can get. "But I'm coming back."

"You are?"

I nod. "I can build furniture anywhere, Easy-Bake. You're here, so that's where I want to be."

Her mouth falls open a little more as she absorbs what I said. Then, she squeals and jumps up, throwing her arms around my neck and slamming her mouth against mine. "Are you serious?"

"That I love you, or I'm moving here?"

"Both, I guess," she replies, still seeming stunned by my words.

"Yes, I'm going to move here. I've already had a conversation with my grandparents about it, and yes, I'm absolutely, one-hundred-percent in love with you. My heart is yours, if you want it."

Her eyes shine with unshed tears as she smiles. "I'll take that heart, because truth be told, you've owned mine for as long as I can remember."

Mine does a wild happy dance in my chest as I grin uncontrollably. "Yeah?"

Joy nods. "I love you too."

The ache I've carried in my chest all day, all week really, seems to just subside instantly with those four little words. My right hand moves up to her hair as I urge, "Say it again."

"I love you," she whispers before punctuating her statement with a kiss.

Our lips fuse together beneath the brisk Christmas night sky. The soft glow of the lights fades away, and all that remains is us.

Joy and me.

Exactly how it was always meant to be.

When we pull apart, she looks up at me with wonder-filled eyes. "You're really coming back?"

"Of course I am," I reassure, wrapping my arm around her shoulder and slowly guiding her back the way we came. "It'll take me a few weeks to wrap up everything back in South Carolina. I have a couple of projects I put off until I was returning so I could come here and help at the farm. Plus, I need to pack up my rental house."

She shakes her head. "I can't believe you're moving here. Just like that."

Stopping, I pull her into my arms once more. "I want to be where you are, Joy. I'm just sorry it's taken me this long to realize it."

She cups my jaw with her soft hand, her fingertips cold against my flesh. "Neither of us could have known. The important part is we know now." Going up on her tiptoes, she presses another intoxicating kiss to my lips. "Just so you know, I would go east with you if you asked."

I shake my head before she's even finished speaking. "Absolutely not. Your business is here. I could never ask you to walk away from that or your family."

She shrugs and rests her cheek against my chest. "I would."

Placing a kiss to her forehead, I reply, "I appreciate that, but no. The only place I want to be is here, and not just because you're here, though that's the main reason. This place is also my home, and I love it. Being back in Snowflake Falls has reminded me of that."

"Well, I admit, I'm relieved I don't have to say goodbye."

I run my hands up and down her arms, trying to make sure she's staying warm. "Just for a short time."

"I can deal with a few weeks, as long as I know you're coming back."

"I promise I'm coming back," I confirm, loving the way she fits so perfectly against my body. I'm not sure how I'm going to deal with not having her with me while I'm gone.

"Where are you going? When you get back?" she asks.

"I'll stay with Gram and Gramps until I find a place. Gramps says I can store my belongings in the barn and his shop for as long as I need."

"I might have a lead for you," she says, her eyes lighting up.

"Yeah?"

Nodding, she bites down on her bottom lip and slips her fingers inside my coat pockets for warmth. "My sister and John are going to rent out his house. He officially moved in with her and Miss Snowflake. They were planning to list it but were wanting to wait until after the first of the year."

"I'd love to talk to them," I tell her, feeling another bubble of excitement in my chest. If I have a place to move into when I return to town that would be even better. Not that I don't want to stay with my grandparents, but I can't pass up an opportunity to potentially move once and be done.

"I'll see them at lunch." Her eyes brighten. "What are you doing tomorrow?"

"Well, I'm supposed to work. I think the biggest job will be keeping Gramps up at the house and not down at the barn, bossing us all around and telling us he can do it better."

She giggles the sweetest sound. "Well, I was going to invite you over for the lunch. Eve and John are going to open presents, and you could talk to them about the house."

"I do appreciate the invite. If we're not too busy, I may take you up on it and stop by."

"I'll get you John's number, and you can discuss details with him."

Slipping my arm around her shoulder once more, we start to head back toward her apartment. "Come on, Easy-Bake. Let's get you back home. As absolutely amazing as this dress looks on you, I must confess, I'm even more curious to see how it looks lying on the floor."

Almost three weeks later

I pull open the door to The Sweet Escape and smile.

There she is.

The woman I love. The one I relocated across the United States to be near. The one I haven't seen in almost three very-long weeks.

Even though we've talked on the phone or sent text messages every day since I left Snowflake Falls to return to South Carolina to pack up my life, it wasn't the same. There was too much distance between us, and I hated every minute of it. That's why I worked hard to wrap up the work I had put off in December and got everything I needed done, so I could leave town a couple of days earlier than planned.

Which is why I'm here.

Joy has no clue.

When we texted earlier, she thought I was just getting ready to pull out of the town I called home for the last fifteen years in my U-Haul, but the truth was, I was already back in Snowflake Falls. I got to town around ten this morning and met John at the house I'll be renting from him.

Fortunately, he was leaving a decent amount of furniture in the house, so I was able to sell a lot of what I didn't need to bring cross country. My personal belongings and all my woodworking tools fill the back of the small trailer, which of course, is sitting in the driveway, waiting to be unloaded. But first, I needed to see the woman I love.

And maybe steal a kiss or two.

I stand at the door, holding the bouquet of flowers. She's finishing up a coffee drink before placing it on the counter. The moment she does, she looks up and our eyes meet. A look of shock transforms to a grin as we just stare at each other for several seconds.

Then, she's moving.

Watching her pace pick up as she makes her way to me gives me plenty of time to brace myself for the impact. Joy leaps at me, crashing into my chest. I'm able to help stabilize her with my left hand without dropping the flowers in my right.

"You're here!" she whisper-yells, her legs wrapping around my waist.

"I'm here," I confirm.

"How? When?"

"I actually had just pulled into town when I talked to you a bit ago. I met John at the house and dropped the trailer."

"I can't believe it. You're really here? To stay?" she asks, and even though we've been over this a dozen times since I left, promising to be back, she still seems shocked by how everything has turned out.

"If you're here, I'm here, Joy. There's nowhere else I want to be."

Then, finally, after nearly three of the longest weeks ever, she presses her lips to mine. The kiss feels like coming home, a culmination of days' worth of packing, selling off furniture, and then traveling. Nineteen days to be exact. And I am ready to be home.

The door opens, the bell chiming throughout the bakery and alerting to a new customer arriving. I release her lips and smile. "You have work to do," I say softly, wishing it were already closing time.

"I do."

With one hand, I slowly help her slide down my body. My cock is hard, but thanks to where she stands, I don't think anyone can bear witness to the extent of my excitement to be back. "These are for you," I state, handing over the bouquet of red roses and white lilies.

"They're gorgeous," she beams, leaning in and inhaling. When she makes eye contact, she asks, "Will you be at the house?"

I nod. "Come on by whenever you're done here."

She glances over her shoulder to the customer approaching the counter. Even though Jan is there to help, she still needs to get back to work. "I could just close up now," she mumbles, making me laugh.

"It's not much longer. Besides, I was going to stop by Feldman's and talk to Tim and Nancy. Gramps said they were interested in selling my furniture pieces when I get back into it." Feldman's is the small furniture store on the square, not too far from the bakery.

"I'm so happy for you."

Gramps is going to let me use his shop too. Sure, I have the small garage I can put some of my tools in for smaller projects, but I'll have a lot more space at the farm. Plus, my family asked me to work at the family farm part time and as needed. During the slower months, I'll be able to spend more time in the shop, doing my thing, but in the busier seasons, I'll help where needed. It's the best of both worlds, and I'm incredibly excited for the opportunity.

"I'll let you get back to it," I tell her, leaning forward and pressing my lips to hers once more.

"More of that later," she states the moment she pulls her mouth away.

"Damn right there will be."

I watch her walk away, placing the flowers on the counter as she gets back to work. She turns around and helps make a drink, while Jan pulls pastries from the glass case.

I don't know how long I stand here and watch her, but I've never felt more settled, more complete in my life. If you would have asked me if returning to Snowflake Falls in the wake of my grandpa's stroke would result in finding the woman I hope to one day spend the rest of my life with, I would have told you to get the hell out of here.

But here I am, completely in love and looking forward to the future.

A future with Joy.

From childhood best friends to hopefully spending our lives together.

I don't know about you, but that sounds pretty damn good to me.

Epilogue

Joy

"Merry Christmas." Burk's lips press against mine, waking me in the best way possible.

Okay, not completely waking me up, since I'm usually a very early riser. My internal clock woke me at four, but I was able to lie in bed and doze back off for a bit, thanks to being in Burk's warm embrace.

"Merry Christmas," I murmur, rolling onto my back and stretching. "Is it time for presents?"

He chuckles and reaches for a steaming coffee mug placed on the nightstand. "It is."

"But first, coffee," I practically sing, sighing after taking my first sip.

Burk isn't a pro but would make a good barista. One of the first things he wanted to do when he moved into this house was learn to make one of my favorite coffee drinks. We started off with a basic coffeepot and eventually moved on to using a milk frother to create delicious lattes.

"Come on, sleepyhead," he says, pulling the comforter back and taking my mug. I slide my feet into my favorite slippers and grab my robe. It's a big fluffy, warm one with sleeping cats all over it. I got it from my sister right before her cat, Miss Snowflake, delivered kittens fathered by John's cat, Biggie.

I reach for my coffee mug and duck into the bathroom. Burk doesn't say a word as I take a minute to pee and brush my teeth. When I'm finally ready, I slip on my warm robe and open the door to find him waiting for me. "All right, let's do this, Burkey Turkey."

He flashes a wide smile and takes my hand. We settle on the floor in the living room so we're close to the tree. It's lit up and looking magnificent, if I do say so myself, and Burk even has Christmas music playing. What's best, the front window shades are open, and you can see the fresh falling snow outside. It's so peaceful and beautiful out there, combined with the coziness and familiarity of the holidays in here.

It's perfect.

"You first," he says, handing over a small, boxed gift.

I rip off the paper and smile at the bottle of my favorite perfume. "Thank you."

"Now you," I state, setting my perfume to the side and reaching for one of his gifts.

Burk dives in, flashing me a grin when he opens a box containing a wood branding iron. When he pulls it out and sees the inscription, his face turns serious. "This is amazing," he informs me, taking in the words. It says 'Handcrafted by Burk Whitman, Snowflake Falls, CO' with an image of his business logo in the middle. "Thank you."

One night over the summer, he mentioned that he saw one online and thought they were cool. He always marks his pieces, but nothing like this. I found someone to custom make this design, and I'm super happy with how it turned out.

Leaning forward, he presses his lips to mine. "I love it."

We continue opening our gifts one by one. I get a few new sweaters, some kitchen gadgets I added to my wish list, and even a new pair of ice skates. Burk opened some clothes, more goodies for his home woodworking shop, and a new winter coat for working at the tree farm.

When he gets to his final gift, I start to get a little nervous. I purchased it on a whim, but now that it's time to give it, I'm not sure what he'll say.

Burk slowly removes the tissue paper from the bag and reaches inside, removing the folded piece of paper from within. He reads over it before his surprised eyes clash with mine. "Seriously?"

I nod, holding my breath as he glances back down and rereads the information.

Does he not like it?

Did I overstep?

What if he doesn't want to go?

My heart is hammering in my chest as I wait for his response.

Another Epilogue

Burk

All I can do is read and reread the words on the paper. I can't believe she did this.

When I look up once more, I see worry filling her stunning green eyes, and I realize she doesn't know how much I love this gift. Setting the paper down, I move to my knees and pull her in for a kiss. "Thank you. I love it."

"Yeah?" she asks, hesitation still evident.

"Absolutely. When do we leave?"

She clears her throat. "New Year's Day."

"I can't wait to show you around and have you see my parents again after all this time," I confirm, excited to return to South Carolina for the first time since moving back to Colorado.

I've thought about going back for a quick visit, but it just didn't work out. My woodworking business took off, especially during the summer. I was making outdoor patio furniture day and night, everything selling before I could even get it on the showroom floor. Then fall hit and the tree farm picked up and has stayed busy through the holidays.

But now we can relax a bit and enjoy a week away.

"You're good with taking the time off from the bakery?" I ask, knowing this is a huge deal for her too.

"I am. I've worked out the details with Jan, and Krista is going to take some paid time off from her job to help too. Plus, Eve and Mom volunteered to work when they can. We'll have a smaller pastry menu that week, and there are no cake orders to worry about. It'll be just fine."

I'm relieved she's been able to get a week's trip away figured out, but more so, I'm excited for her to see my parents. They've talked on video chat and Joy and my mom text, but this will be their first time meeting face-to-face, since we've been together.

The lines of communication have remained open between my parents and grandparents too. Over the last year, a lot of phone calls have been made and a lot of talking has taken place. I'm certain an in-person visit will happen with them soon too, as long as they continue to talk and take steps to repair their damaged relationship.

"Thank you for this," I tell her before sliding my hands into her hair and moving forward to kiss her lips once more. I'll never get tired of kissing her. Her mouth was made for mine.

"You're welcome," she replies when we finally come up for air. "And thank you for my gifts too. I love them all."

"I have one more for you," I reply, my heart rate starting to climb.

This is it.

"You do?" she asks, glancing under the empty tree, but I know she won't outwardly see the last gift there.

"I do," I confirm. "It's in the tree."

Her eyebrows draw together as confusion sweeps across her angelic face. "*In* the tree?"

"Well, on it. See if you can find it."

She climbs off the floor and stares at the tree we spent so much time decorating. She still has a tree over at her apartment, but I don't think it's been on but one or two nights since we put it up. She's been staying with me here, at my house, more times than not, which is exactly how I want it. I want her here every night from this one moving forward.

I know immediately when she spots the extra ornament I hung on the tree early this morning while she was still sleeping. She smiles and reaches for the small trinket box I made. I swear I'm not breathing as she runs her finger across the top of the new ornament on our tree.

"I thought we could start a new tradition," I tell her, causing her to look my way. "We hang a new ornament on the tree each year to signify something important that happened that year."

She smiles down at the square. "I love our first one."

I engraved a few different items on the small box. A cupcake on one side, a bare tree on the other to signify our jobs. The front has the year, and the top a pair of ice skates.

"It's beautiful."

"Open it."

Joy looks back down at the box and gently lifts the top. I get into position and smile when she gasps. She spins to the side, her head volleying between the diamond ring inside the box and me on one knee.

"You've been my best friend for as long as I can remember. Every single memory I have in Snowflake Falls features you, and I want you in every single one moving forward." I take a deep breath and ask the most important question of my life. "Joy Campbell, will you marry me?"

She smiles through her tears as she nods emphatically. "Yes. Yes, I'll marry you."

I reach for the box and pull out the ring, my fingers shaking as I slide it on her hand.

It's a perfect fit.

Just like her and me.

When the ring is on her hand, I stand up and kiss my fiancée. Her hands rest on the sides of my face, and even though I can't see it, I feel the weight of that ring adorning her left hand. "I love you," I whisper against her lips.

"I love you too."

She pulls back and smiles down at the solitaire princess cut diamond ring. It's not huge or extravagant. I know Joy wouldn't want that. It's timeless and breathtaking and looks amazing on her hand. "I can't believe this," she whispers.

"Believe it, Easy-Bake. Or should I call you Mrs. Easy-Bake Whitman."

She barks out a laugh. "I think that would look perfect embroidered on an apron."

"Done," I reply, making a mental note to get that ordered ASAP. "Now, let's get ready to go."

She makes a face. As far as she knows, we're not going anywhere until lunchtime, but that was all part of the plan. "Where?"

"Your sister's," I tell her, pretty proud of myself for keeping this secret. "Everyone's there waiting."

"What?"

"Lunch is actually brunch, and everyone will be there. Your parents, John and Eve, and my grandparents. We're going to celebrate John and Eve's first anniversary, but also our engagement."

She snorts and shakes her head. "Pretty sure of yourself that I'd say yes, huh?"

"Well, I'll admit, I was a little nervous, but I was very hopeful."

She steps into my embrace and rises on her tiptoes. "I would always say yes to you, Burkey Turkey. Always."

"Always, huh?" I ask, waggling my eyebrows suggestively. "We do have a little time before we need to be next door."

She giggles and slides her hands down my chest. I grow hard instantly, before her hands have a chance to wrap around me. "Always a yes."

Picking her up, I throw her over my shoulder. Her laughter fills the air as I practically run back to the bedroom, slapping her ass as I go. It's not hard, especially with pajamas and a robe covering her, but it gets a response, nonetheless.

"You're gonna pay for that," she hollers.

I carefully set her down on the floor and frame her face with my hands. She covers mine with her own, the diamond sparkling like the bright white lights on the Christmas tree. "I have no doubt about it."

Then, I claim her mouth with mine, cementing her in my heart forever.

My best friend.

The woman I love.

My future.

For eternity.

THE END

Did you miss Eve and John's story? You can grab your copy of Merry Little Mix-Up, Snowflake Falls book 1.

Don't miss a single reveal, release, or sale! Sign up for my newsletter.

http://www.laceyblackbooks.com/newsletter

Books Also by Lacey Black

Rivers Edge series

Trust Me, Rivers Edge book 1 (Maddox and Avery) – FREE at all retailers

Fight Me, Rivers Edge book 2 (Jake and Erin)

Expect Me, Rivers Edge book 3 (Travis and Josselyn)

Promise Me: A Novella, Rivers Edge book 3.5 (Jase and Holly)

Protect Me, Rivers Edge book 4 (Nate and Lia)

Boss Me, Rivers Edge book 5 (Will and Carmen)

Trust Us: A Rivers Edge Christmas Novella (Maddox and Avery)
> *~ This novella was originally part of the Christmas Miracles Anthology*

With Me, A Rivers Edge Christmas Novella (Brooklyn and Becker)

Bound Together series

Submerged, Bound Together book 1 (Blake and Carly)

Profited, Bound Together book 2 (Reid and Dani)

Entwined, Bound Together book 3 (Luke and Sidney)

Summer Sisters series

My Kinda Kisses, Summer Sisters book 1 (Jaime and Ryan)

My Kinda Night, Summer Sisters book 2 (Payton and Dean)

My Kinda Song, Summer Sisters book 3 (Abby and Levi)

My Kinda Mess, Summer Sisters book 4 (Lexi and Linkin)

My Kinda Player, Summer Sisters book 5 (AJ and Sawyer)

My Kinda Player, Summer Sisters book 6 (Meghan and Nick)

My Kinda Wedding, A Summer Sisters Novella book 7 (Meghan and Nick)

Rockland Falls series

Love and Pancakes, Rockland Falls book 1
Love and Lingerie, Rockland Falls book 2
Love and Landscape, Rockland Falls book 3
Love and Neckties, Rockland Falls book 4

Standalone
Music Notes, a sexy contemporary romance standalone
A Place To Call Home, a Memorial Day novella
Exes and Ho Ho Ho's, a sexy contemporary romance standalone novella
Pants on Fire
Double Dog Dare You
Grip
Bachelor Swap, A Bachelor Tower Series Novel
Perfect Kiss, Mason Creek Series book 9
Waiting For Love, The Love Vixen Series book 11
Quarterback Keeper, a surprise baby novella
Kissing A Stranger, book 4 in the multi-author The Kissing Games series

Burgers and Brew Crüe Series
Kickstart My Heart, book 1
Don't Go Away Mad, book 2
Same Ol' Situation, book 3
Wild Side, book 4
What's It Gonna Take, book 5
Home Sweet Home, book 6
Too Young to Fall in Love, book 7
Without You, book 8
Time For Change, book 9
You're All I Need, book 10

Pine Village Series
Pretty Remarkable, a free prequel short story
Pretty Incredible, book 1
Pretty Dependable, book 2
Pretty Drunk, book 3
Pretty Relentless, book 4
Pretty Wild, book 5
Pretty Desperate, book 6

Co-Written with *NYT Bestselling* Author, Kaylee Ryan
It's Not Over, Fair Lakes book 1
Just Getting Started, Fair Lakes book 2
Can't Get Enough, Fair Lakes book 3
Fair Lakes Box Set
Boy Trouble
Home To You, a second chance novella
Beneath the Fallen Stars, Never Too Far book 1
Beneath the Desert Sun, Never Too Far book 2
Tell Me A Story
Royal
Crying Shame
Watch and Learn

About the Author

USA Today Bestselling Author Lacey Black is a Midwestern girl with a passion for reading, writing, and shopping. She carries her e-reader with her everywhere she goes so she never misses an opportunity to read a few pages. Always looking for a happily ever after, Lacey is passionate about contemporary romance novels and enjoys it further when you mix in a little suspense. She resides in a small town in Illinois with her husband and two children.

Website: www.laceyblackbooks.com

Email: laceyblackwrites@gmail.com

Newsletter: http://www.laceyblackbooks.com/newsletter

www.ingramcontent.com/pod-product-compliance
Lightning Source LLC
Chambersburg PA
CBHW060644260626
47161CB00008B/2998

* 9 7 8 1 9 5 1 8 2 9 6 9 8 *